author's note

This is a work of fiction. Names, characters, places, and incidents either are the product of the author's imagination or are used fictitiously, and any resemblance to actual persons, living or dead, events, or locales is entirely coincidental.

dedication

I dedicate my first novel to two people who have been a huge influence on my life. They have been my teachers, guidance counselors, pillars of strength and, most importantly, my best friends, Jesse and Wallace Wright. Mom and Dad, thank you for being so proud of me and loving me unconditionally. I love you both.

To Lourdes DeLeon Davis-Tilles, Hortence Dennis White and Ethel Davis Cartwright, I feel you in my heart and I talk with you in my dreams. I miss you all.

Lastly, I never imagined having to type this. To my sister-in-law, Sandra Coles-Lipscomb, who went home on July 23, 2002. My heart is heavy and my mind is confused. I constantly ask, "why?"You will suffer no more. You were loved and you will be truly missed. Rest in peace, Sis.

acknowledgements

I am forever grateful to everyone who provided me with the love, guidance, understanding and support to write my first novel: my husband, Victor, I couldn't have done this without you; my editor and road dawg, Jo Hawley Chubbs; Darlene Rowe-Stukes, for assisting me with my publicity and promotions; Teresa Clark, Shari L. McCoy and Glenda Barlow for reading the chapters and keeping me on the right track; Nellie Graham, Linda McIntosh, Quintina Butereza, Lori Lee, Kathy Queen, Denise Touissant and Joe Wright, thank you for your excitement and valuable input; Adrian Long, who told me two years ago that I should turn my short story into a novel; my brother Herbert Lipscomb, who still can't believe it— this one's for you; my sisters, Jacqueline Johnson, Valerie Lowen, Colleen Green and Sheila Wright; my nieces, nephews, and a host of family and friends—I hope the words within these pages do not embarrass you too much; Collen Dixon, author of *Simon Says*, and Brenda L. Thomas, author of *Threesome*, for their advice and support and allowing me to pick their brains; and last, but always first in my heart, Leslie K. Martin, my voice of reasoning, my big sister, best friend and confidant, thank you for always being in my corner. If I left anyone out, please, blame it on my mind and not my heart.

— J.T.

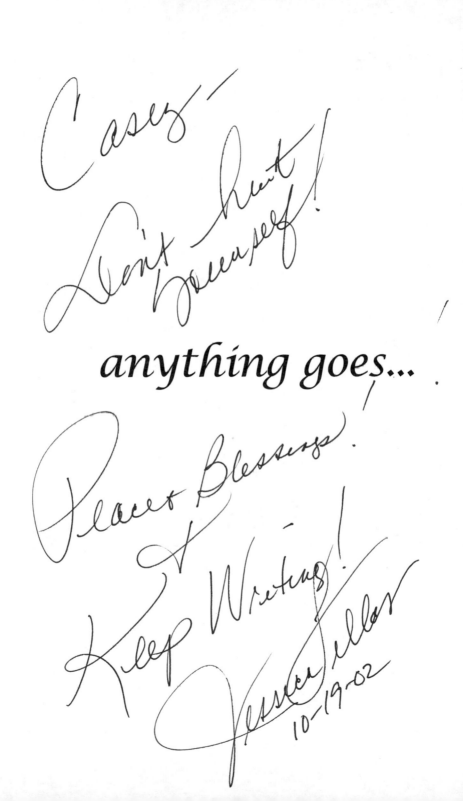

Casey —

Don't hurt yourself!

anything goes...

Peace + Blessings

Keep Writing!

Jessica Silber
10-19-02

1 / a ray of sunshine

The only thing I have shopped for in the past week or so is underwear. Living the single life doesn't leave much room for doing laundry. My sister told me I was just trifling and needed to slow my ass down so that I could, at least, have a pair of clean panties! But, little does she know, baby sister don't wear panties. I believe in easy access. I never know when I have to lift my skirt and take care of some business.

My friends call me Ray, short for a Ray of Sunshine, because I am always spontaneous, witty, charming, loving, fun, intelligent, diversified and I love to live life to the fullest. I set no limitations on myself. I know what I want and where I want to be in life. I love old school and R&B, with a touch of Jazz. I am your chocolate girl who will make a smile down inside you between the sheets.

I would like to meet someone who is very secure and confident, gentle, kind, respectful, sincere, honest and loves to have fun. He must be very spontaneous in every aspect of life, especially when I want some dick. He can't have any hang-ups or drama. Drama leads to stress, stress leads to tears, and I don't have any plans, whatsoever, of shedding any tears.

Nice single's ad, huh? My ass is still fucking single too. I am beautiful as hell, have a body to die for and a pussy with a serious attitude. I don't get it. Brothers are always saying there aren't any good black women around, just so they can make a beeline to the great Milky Way — no offense to the candy bar. Black men need to stop using black women as an excuse to fuck white women. If being with a white woman is the preference of a black man, then he needs to own up to that. But don't claim that it is the black woman's fault because he chooses to be with a white woman — saying that we are difficult to deal with. Shoot, we aren't difficult; we just don't put up with the bullshit that most black men dish out. It seems to me like brothers are doing their mothers an injustice. After all, isn't she a black woman? Oh, I guess it's her fault too, huh?

Personally, I believe that black women are the strongest of the human species and some brothers can't handle that shit, especially that brother who prefers to remain on top. Hell, when it comes to sex, we will roll with every stroke. And when we are finished, the brother don't do shit but whine "don't touch me," roll the fuck over and go to sleep. I had this one brother to stick his damn thumb in his mouth after he pulled it from my ass, the nasty bastard.

A white woman can have his nasty ass. Hell, let a sister on top, and you will forget to pay your rent. Sisters aren't doormats. When we are on our backs, do you see a welcome mat on our pussies? Now, don't get me wrong, I am not saying that white women are doormats — well, not all of them — but, they do put up with a lot of bullshit that black men dish out. Sisters don't tolerate that shit because we recognize the fact that we are the black man's backbone; they came from us, didn't they? Shit, we prefer to be on top with them telling us whose dick it is. Why must brothers always perpetrate?

2 / all day groovin'

Ramone is fine as hell with caramel skin, hazel eyes and a body that reminds me of those male dancers I've seen performing every Tuesday night at the Classics Night Club. The brother has it going on in the basement and on the first floor, but in the attic, he ain't got shit. You know, one of those "all-they-can-do-is-fuck-me" brothers. I am not going to lie, Ramone tried to knock a hole in my pussy and I enjoyed every stroke. To my recollection, he is the best lover that I have experienced and I am keeping him in my back pocket for 'just in case' purposes.

I met Ramone at a pool party a few years back. It was hot as shit that day too. I was dressed in a pair of bootie shorts, that showed my ass cheeks, and a thin-as-gauze halter top. My high-beamed nipples happily greeted folks each time the breeze kissed them. My hair was pinned up and my makeup was flawless. The music was pumping, liquor was flowing and food was burning on the grill.

"Damn that smells good," Ramone said, inhaling the essence of what I thought was me.

"Thank you. It's a body oil I created." I turned to face the most beautiful eyes I've ever seen on a man, not to mention those big sensuous lips.

"Naw baby, I was talking about the hamburgers and hotdogs. Hook me up and put everything on it." I didn't hear a damn word he said, because I was daydreaming about what those big lips would feel like caressing my clit. "Hello."

I shifted my weight from my right to my left. "Um, oh, yes. I'm sorry, what did you say?"

Ramone balanced a basketball between his arm and hip, with beads of sweat dancing on his forehead. "Hook me up a burger with everything on it."

"Is that right? Well, you can have it any way you want when you fix it your damn self."

"Oh, my bad, Boo. I thought you were the chef. You standing here flipping burgers..." he smugly said, while looking me up and down.

I rolled my eyes and said, "Whatever." "Do you like what you see?" I knew that he did, but hell, I like having my ego stroked.

He licked those suckable lips. "Yes, as a matter of fact I do." Damn, he is going to make me cum on myself.

"So, beautiful, are you attached?"

"No, I'm not attached. But, I do have friends."

"Friends?"

"So what, you have a hearing disorder? Yes, I said friends."

"Naw, I ain't got no hearing disorder. I hear just fine. What kind of friends?"

I folded my arms across my chest. "What kind of question is that?"

"A question that requires a very simple answer."

There he goes again, tantalizing me with those damn lips. I wish he would cut that shit out. "You need to rephrase your question so it don't sound like you all up in a sista's business, brotha." I turned my attention back to the grill.

"Okay. These friends of yours, are they friends you fuck or friends you shoot the shit with?"

I turned to face him with one hand on my hip and waving the spatula I was using to flip the burgers with in his face. "That's none of your damn business, first of all. Secondly, I don't have time for this shit. I don't play games and I don't play with boys…"

"Boys? Do I look like a damn *boy* to you?" he snarled with the quickness. That was an easy question to answer. Only a man could bring me to moisture, and right now this man has me overly moist. But, I wouldn't give him the satisfaction of knowing this bit of information.

"Whatever." I rolled my eyes and returned to the task of flipping the burgers, refusing to give him a response that would enlarge his ego more.

He takes a step closer. "Damn baby, why does it have to be like that?" His breath smelled minty and felt good on my neck.

Facing him and catching a whiff of his Cool Water cologne, "Be like what? Look, um, whatever your name is…"

"Ramone. My name is Ramone Jarvis."

"Well, Ramone Jarvis, I don't have time for games. If you see what you like, then we can talk. I sure as hell like what I see." I could not believe the words that had just jumped out of my mouth.

He grabbed his crotch. "Yeah, yeah, for sure, I like what I see."

Typically, the grabbing of one's crotch would have turned me off. But, he looked so damn sexy doing it and I just couldn't seem to get my mind off of those sensuous lips wrapped around my clit. So I let that trifling shit slide.

"Cool. So handsome, are you attached?" I held my breath.

"Single as a one-dollar-bill, baby," he chuckled, obviously thinking that what he said was funny.

Smiling and thinking that there is a God, "Cool."

"Cool." Damn, is there an echo out here? Why does he keep repeating what I say?

"So, beautiful, I didn't catch your name."

"I never threw it."

He started stroking my cheek with his thumb. "Oh, a sense of humor. I like that in my women."

I smacked his hand away from my face. "Don't be puttin' your funky ass hands in my damn face. Your women? How many women do you have?"

"Damn girl, why you so hard on a brotha?"

With my hands on my hips, I persisted. "You need to answer my question."

"Just like you have friends, I have friends too," he mimicked.

Mocking him with the same sarcasm he showed me, "Oh, I see. Are they friends you fuck or friends you shoot the shit with?"

"You got me. I deserved that. So, your name?"

"What about my name, you writing me a check?"

"Oh, I see. You're the type who likes to play games too. Like you, I don't play with little girls." Ramone turned on his heels to walk away.

"Fuck you!"

He turned to face me. "Sure, but don't you think I should at least know your name before I stick my dick in you?"

I smiled at his humor. "You got jokes. My name is Raven."

"Raven," he said gently, as though he was using my name as if it were my clit, caressing it with those sensuous lips. Damn, I really need to get a grip. "Raven is a beautiful name."

"I'm sure my mama and daddy would appreciate you liking my name."

"Just like the bird," he said with a mouth full of hamburger.

Damn, he could've swallowed before he opened his mouth. He must've left his manners at home. Now I'm getting pissed and my coochie is drying out. "Damn, thanks for the compliment," I snapped. "A raven is a big black bird that hovers over road kill waiting to consume it!"

"Naw Honey Dip, that's not what I mean and you know it."

"Well, what exactly do you mean, Honey dip?"

While working on his second hamburger, he said, "What I should've said was your name is as beautiful as you are."

Damn, I hope he can devour me the way he's devouring those damn hamburgers. "Whatever."

Ramone looks like he is about to choke. "Look, I'm sorry." He still has a mouth full of food. "Let me make it up to you."

Somebody get this man some water! I am getting more and more irritated and I make a mental note to never take this man out to eat in public. "I don't need you to make it up to me. You need to stop stuffing your face like this shit is your last meal before you choke to death, because you will choke to death. I don't know how to perform the Heimlich maneuver, nor do I know CPR!"

"Oh, so you got more jokes," he said, inhaling his third hamburger. Damn this is one greedy motherfucker.

Retrieving my ink pen from my purse, I take the palm of his hand and begin to write my phone number. "Listen, here is my number…Ramone, is it? Give me a call and maybe we can hook up and catch a movie or something."

"Sounds like a plan," he said, smiling like the cat that swallowed the canary.

Turning on my heels to walk away, I look over my shoulder and I say, with a smile, "Yeah, whatever."

Knowing that he is watching me, I give him something to really look at. Bending over to tighten the strap on my sandals, I give Ramone an eye full of nothing but ass. I catch a glimpse of my watch. Damn, look at the time. I've got thirty minutes to meet Morgan. I've wasted too much time with Ramone, the idiot. But, he was sexy as hell, had something to offer and I intended on finding out exactly what it was.

3 / you don't miss your water 'til your well runs dry

I had taken a shower and washed my hair before bed. I was hoping that if Arthur felt the urge to rest his hands between my legs, he would notice that I was not wearing any panties and that I was ready to explode just by his touch. I so badly wanted a repeat performance of last week. I didn't know that my body was so flexible. Where did he learn all of that stuff? Probably from all of those porn tapes he keeps hidden under the sofa in the basement. Humph, I don't care so long as he doesn't stop doing it!

It's been nine months since we've been back together. A year ago we decided to call it quits. We were having some serious struggles within our marriage. The biggest problem was communication, which led to arguing and physical altercations, which led to Raven aiming her .22-caliber at Arthur's temple. That girl scared the shit out of me. Raven had Arthur shaking in his skin so bad, he pissed his pants. Personally, I thought she was crazy enough to pull the trigger. Arthur should have known better than to put his hands on me when I have Raven for a sister. Some people just never learn.

After a few months of being separated, I realized that I truly loved Arthur and I wanted to make our marriage work. I'd thought about dating, but that thought was shot to hell when I met this guy in the grocery store. He wasn't bad looking. However, unlike Raven, I don't weigh too much on how men look or what's hiding behind zipper number one, but the warmth of their heart and the content of their soul. So, when I attempted to date this guy, I tried to measure his heart and his soul by Arthur's, and well, let's just say that I never got the opportunity to see what was behind zipper number one. I probably would have been disappointed.

Just nine months ago, I 'd been thinking of how I was going to get my husband back. Arthur had his mind set that he didn't want to go through the emotional roller coaster again. He was seeing someone else. At least that's what I thought, but I didn't have any real proof. I do know that he contacted an 'old friend' who had the biggest crush on him before we met. Of course he was oblivious to it all, but being a woman, I didn't miss a beat with old girl. It's all good because, in the end, I came out on top. Arthur says that he and this 'old friend' went to church and that was it, so he says. He has never lied to me before, so there's no reason why I shouldn't believe him now. But, there is always a first time for everything.

Arthur is always so honest, sometimes too damn honest, if you ask me. Some things you just need to keep to yourself. Nevertheless, being a liar is not one of his specialties, and besides, he's not very good in the fibbing department. As a matter of fact, I doubt if he even looks at other women. Then again, I'm no fool, that's for sure.

But, throughout those nine months, I was determined to figure out how I was going to get him back. Out of all of the books I have read, I can't believe that nothing comes to mind. Well if I was going to do this, I had to do it on my own, and I did just that.

My Dearest Arthur,

It takes a minute to have a crush on someone, an hour to like someone, and a day to love someone. But it takes a lifetime to forget someone. I want to spend my lifetime loving you, admiring you, appreciating you, respecting you, caring for you, enjoying you, hearing you grind your teeth at night, watching you sleep, being a friend to you, being your lover, being the mother of your children, being your wife. I know we cannot undo all of the hurt and pain that has transpired over the years. However, we can put it behind us, learn from it, move forward, and live a loving, caring, prosperous life.

I love you so much. I didn't realize how much I loved you and how much I am still in love with you until I had to lay in a cold bed, alone, yearning for you to be near me and wanting to hear your voice. I miss you waiting until I've fallen fast asleep to turn the television. I miss hearing my nicknames—honey, baby and pookie.

They say you don't miss your water until your well runs dry; I am so thirsty and only you can quench my thirst. I have done a lot of soul-searching and self-exploring. I guess it's all of those books I've read. From reading those books, I have also learned a lot about my choices and myself. I choose to be plural rather than singular.

I think this separation has changed us both for the better. It gave us both a chance to look inside and discover new things about ourselves. Now, we communicate on a more advanced level and can see our wrongs and are able to right them.

I love you baby and I will spend the rest of my life proving my love to you. I can't promise you that my ugly side will not rear its head, on occasions. However, your patience, care, love and understanding that I am human, is all I need. I want to be Mrs. Arthur Carrington, once again. I need my better half. I am not whole without you.

Loving you forever,

Morgan

A week later, I was home, in my bed, rocking my man's world. We had sex in every room of the house. And today, we enjoy the night air while exchanging love juices on our deck.

"Hey honey, you still up?"

"Uh huh." I pulled the covers back and patted his pillow. "I'm waiting on you."

"That's good to hear 'cause I have something for you." Arthur allowed his boxers to drop to this ankles, then stepped out of them.

"Damn, Arthur!" I sat up in the bed and pulled the covers up around my neck.

"What's wrong?"

"What the hell is that?"

"My dick?"

"No, I'm talking about those big black beads you have dangling from your butt."

Arthur laughed at my ignorance. "Anal beads."

I looked at him like he was a stranger standing before me. "Okay. What do you plan to do with those?"

"They are anal beads, Morgan."

"Yeah, I got that part. How did you get them in your butt?"

"Well, I thought we could try something new."

"I don't know what has gotten into you, but…"

"Nothing has gotten into me, Morgan."

"Yes, something has gotten into to you. I think you've been watching too many porn tapes."

"Morgan, I am only trying to heighten our sexuality."

"You want to tell me how sticking big black beads in your butt, heightens your sexuality?"

"Morgan…"

"That stuff looks painful."

"Oh, but its not, baby." Arthur turned his back towards me and bent over, exposing a string of beads hanging from his rectum. "See, there's nothing to it."

"Oh my God!" I scooted down in the bed and pulled the covers over my face. "Arthur Carrington, you take those things out right this minute!"

"You do it for me, Morgan."

"What?"

"I want you to pull them out."

I raised up in the bed, yanked the covers off of me and stood to my feet. "Arthur, that is some gay shit and I ain't interested."

"Morgan, baby, please, do this for us. I want to try new things with you. I want us to broaden our sexual horizons."

"Fine. Turn around."

Arthur turned around and bent over. His beautiful mocha-colored tail was glaring at me with damn anal beads dangling, looking like a chain attached to an ass lamp. "Are you sure you want me to do this?" I reached for the beads and closed my eyes.

"Yes, I am sure. Be...ouch, Morgan!"

"What?"

"You know what," he shouted.

"I did what you told me to do."

"Yes, but I didn't tell you to yank my damn hemorrhoids out either!" Arthur stormed off to the bathroom, slammed the door and I went to bed.

4 / my house, my rules

It's an unusually cool night to be the end of August. My bedroom windows are open; a gentle breeze is blowing through, caressing the pastel cotton and silk veils that drape around the frame of my canopy bed. Matching jade-colored stucco walls are the canvass for my boudoir. Coordinating drapes, which mirror the canopy veils that caress my bed, billow and wave around each window frame. In other words, all my shit matches. Candles illuminate from my matching Victorian-style dresser and nightstand. The satin sheets on my bed hold all of my secrets that should remain just that, a damn secret!

Tonight is the night. I finally get to meet Michael Anthony. We've been chatting on the Internet for close to two months now. I still can't believe he is driving from Cleveland, Ohio to Washington, D.C., just to see me. Hell, I can't believe I invited some stranger from the Internet to come and stay the weekend at my house. Well, actually, he invited himself. What the fuck was I thinking? I have seen too many Internet-based relationships get flushed straight down the toilet of love with the rest of the shit and I am not trying to go that route. Michael seems to be a really nice guy and I've been talking shit with him every night. Getting scared now is useless. Besides, he just finished graduate school and is about to start his own business, so he says. Maybe he is Mr. Right. Who knows? We will see. All I know is that I have read some horror stories about people meeting and dating from the Internet. Most of the people aren't who they are claiming to be just so they can get a piece of ass. But, if this brother isn't who he says he is, he will be sorry he fucked with me. I don't play that shit.

I met Michael in a single's chat room for black folks that are over forty years old. Although I am only twenty-seven, I prefer to dialogue with folks older than myself. I learn a lot from older folks. Besides, I remember my mama telling me that the only thing you can learn from folks your age is to not repeat their mistakes. I prefer older men—what Morgan says about older men ain't true, I have yet to get worms. Older men are much more experienced, not to mention, more mature than men my age, especially with the clit. I believe older men have had plenty of time and have been on enough clits to master the art of clit sucking.

I have this fascination with my clit. Once, this guy told me, while he had me in his mouth, that I had the prettiest clit that he's ever seen. So, of course, I had to check it out for myself. After he left my place, I headed for the bathroom, dropped my panties to my ankles, sat on the toilet and grabbed the mirror that was propped against the wall on the sink. Spreading my legs apart, I positioned the mirror between my legs to take a look. Well, either I had a plump, juicy clit or homeboy sucked my clit until it was twice its original size! Seeing my clit the size of a large red grape scared the hell out of me. I promised myself that any man who has not received his Ph.D. in the art of clit sucking would never, ever get close to Clitina again; especially brothers with small thin lips who use their teeth, which is why I stay away from white men. Don't get me wrong, I have nothing against white men, I just prefer big, suckable lips. Clitina was sore for a good week and that night was the last time that brother saw my clit or me. Thank goodness I used a condom that gave me great protection; his dick was the size of a baby carrot. When he pulled out, the condom stayed in place. I've really got to be more selective.

Last month, my phone bill was so damn high, I almost suffered a nose bleed. I know Michael's phone bill is not half the amount mine is, because I am always calling him. Except for that time he called me, collect, saying he was out with his boys, was thinking about me and decided to call me from a pay phone. I was glad he was thinking about me, but I would have appreciated him thinking about me—using his cell phone or waiting until his ass got home—instead of calling me collect. I don't know what it is about this man that keeps me so excited, but I surely intend to find out tonight.

Michael phoned me at five o'clock this morning, saying that he would arrive some time around midnight and it's eleven o'clock now. I better get myself ready. Please let this man look like that fine ass picture he sent me. I know about people sending pictures of a relative or a picture scanned from a magazine and try to pass them off as themselves. I am embarrassed to say that I fell for that shit once.

I met this brother online, he seemed real cool and we had a lot in common. Well, the only thing we didn't have in common was the fact that he was a lying ass son-of-a-biscuit-eater. We made plans for him to fly into D.C. to spend Labor Day weekend with me. We decided to wear red so that we would be able to recognize one another once he exited the plane. Well, something didn't sit right with me about this guy. For one, all I had was a pager number and two, he claimed not to be married. So, instead of wearing red, I wore black and I stood in the wings so I wouldn't be noticed. Well, just as the sky is blue, this brother was about five-feet-five inches tall, weighing in at a hefty three hundred pounds, munching on a powdered donut. He wore a red shirt, red jeans and red canvas tennis shoes trimmed with white rubber and white shoe strings that were way too long, because he tripped, fell into the wall and all of his bags hit the floor. This was not the face nor the body that popped up in my email box. I guess it should've clicked that he was a tub-o-lard when he sent me a picture that favored someone I'd seen on the cover of GQ magazine. I ran from where I was standing like I had stolen something and vowed to never do that shit again. But now, look at my ass, waiting for another buster I met from the Internet. Vows do get broken from time to time.

Glancing at the wood-framed clock with an inset of African artwork hanging on my bedroom wall, I see that I have time for a hot bath and a soothing glass of Chardonnay. When Michael informed me that he would be visiting me for the weekend, I quickly called a cleaning service, so my place is spotless. Hell, when I got the bill, I decided to eat off the damn floor. I can't believe they charged me two hundred and fifty dollars just to clean a one-bedroom condo. It's small, but it's mine. It's not as fancy as Morgan's home—vaulted ceilings, twenty-foot floor-to-ceiling windows, two lofts and a sitting room off from her bedroom that is as big as my condo. Now, that girl is the one who needs a cleaning service, especially with wall-to-wall white carpeting. I refuse to clean that much house. But, she loves it and, not to mention, she is just plain cheap. Arthur sold their first house and purchased this mini castle for them to make a fresh start after they rekindled their broken down marriage. I'm happy for Morgan. Sometimes, I wish it were me, instead of her.

"Ah, this feels nice." I said aloud, immersing myself into a not-too-hot bubble bath, as if waiting for a response from my neighbors through these paper-thin walls. Mental note, don't fuck in the bathroom. Damn, now the phone rings once I've gotten settled. I knew I should've installed a phone line in this bathroom when I had the chance. "Coming!" I yelled as though the phone could understand or respond. I glance at my caller ID and recognize the number. Snatching the phone from the cradle, "Girl, this better be good."

"Hey Whorina, you busy?"

I snatched a towel from the towel rack and wrapped it around me. "Morgan, kiss my ass with that Whorina shit. I'm soaking in the tub."

"This time of night?"

"Yeah. I'm expecting a house guest."

"Damn, who is he this time?"

"Mo, why don't you get some business of your own and stay out of mine, please? Where is your husband? Ask his rich ass to buy you some damn business."

"Okay, okay. Damn. I can't help it if I can't keep up with your many whorish escapades. It does get confusing. Maybe I need to keep a tracking log." She broke into laughter.

I resist the urge to reach out and touch her ass. "Do you remember the guy I've been chatting with on the Internet? I told you about him."

"Uh huh, someone named Anthony?"

"His name is Michael Anthony."

"Yeah, I remember. Not again, Ray. Are you a glutton for punishment?"

Since I am not in the mood to curse this bitch out, I ignore her sarcasm. "He will be here around midnight—coming in from Cleveland, Ohio for the weekend."

"Cleveland, Ohio?"

"Morgan, is there something wrong with your damn phone?"

"I don't think so, why?

"Forget it, Mo."

"Oh, okay. Well where is Anthony staying?"

"Michael. His name is Michael and he is staying with me."

"Who are you getting pissy with? It's not my fault his mother was high when she named him."

"I happen to like this name. It sounds regal."

"He's probably ghetto, and do you think that's a good idea to let him stay with you? I mean, don't you listen to the news? You don't know him from a hill of beans. He may be a rapist or an axe murderer or something like that," she scolded, being her overly concerned self. "I don't want to get a call from your neighbors telling me that there's a strange odor coming from your place, because this Anthony guy has chopped your ass up in a million pieces."

Morgan can get on my last nerve with her dramatic ass, but she means well.

"Mo, I can take care of myself and I do know how to dial 9-1-1 if he shows his ass. Besides, have you forgotten about my .22-caliber that I have under my bed? You know I will use that bitch."

"Fine. Can't nobody tell your ass shit. Just promise me you will be careful."

"I will. Hey, why did you call me in the first place?"

"Nothing." She took a deep sigh. "Just making my nightly call."

"Kind of late for you, isn't it?"

"I didn't know I couldn't call you after a certain hour," she snapped.

"Bitch, that is not what I meant and you know it. Is everything alright with you and Arthur?"

"Arthur and I are just fine, Sluttisha. Why do you ask?"

"Well, you are acting like booty right now." We both giggled like a couple of school girls.

"See, that's why I love you, Ray. You keep me in stitches."

"Yeah, I love you too."

"Call me tomorrow."

"I will. Tell Arthur I said hello. Bye."

"Okay, I will. Bye-bye sweetie. Have fun, but most importantly, please be careful."

"I will."

Morgan has issues and I love her dearly. A girl couldn't ask for a better sister. Well, that is, when she ain't all up in my business. I can't move without her asking what, when, where, who, why and how. The girl missed her calling. Instead of being an office manager, she should've been a damn reporter. But, I must admit, there is a slight bit of envy on my part. She has the perfect life with a husband who loves her dirty drawers; now that is some serious love. He has his own medical practice, of which she manages, and a big, beautiful home in suburban Maryland. For as long as I can remember, I have been trying to model myself after her. I love everything about her. I love being around her and smelling her. Everything around her has to be perfect, down to her heavily starched uniforms that she doesn't have to wear everyday. But, she says that she is a team player and just because her husband is the head physician, and owns the practice, doesn't mean that she is better than or should stand out from anyone else. I think it's because she doesn't want the employees to think she is some high and mighty bitch that feels she can get away with whatever she wants, just because her hubby owns the place. Yeah, that's my girl, but she knows entirely too much of my business. It's a good thing I am not a celebrity. She would be in blackmail heaven and, not to mention, getting rich from me paying her hush money.

While walking to the hall linen closet to grab a bottle of vinegar and water douche and my pear-scented body lotion, the phone rings again. It's probably Michael calling to tell me that he is lost or something.

"Hi sweetie, are you getting close?"

"Didn't know you were expecting me, Ray."

Damn, why didn't I check the caller ID? "Ramone, hey baby. What's up?"

"I want to come over. I feel like breaking your back tonight."

Being quick on my feet, but making sure that I don't give Ramone the idea that I have other plans. "Baby, I would love to have you breaking my back tonight, but I can't sweetie. Morgan is over and we are doing girlie stuff tonight."

"Damn, alright then. I will just have to take a cold shower and stroke my own dick tonight."

"You do that and I promise to make it up to you. I've got to run baby. I will call you tomorrow, okay?" Knowing Ramone, he will insist on showing up and want to do a damn threesome with my sister and me.

"Okay baby. Call me tomorrow so we can make plans."

My call waiting beeps in my ear. "Okay baby, there's my other line. I will call you tomorrow. Bye." I quickly switched over to the other line before he could respond.

"Hello."

"Hey Ray, it's me," came from Michael's tired sounding voice over the crackling of his cell phone.

"Where are you?"

"I'm not far, but I think I'm turned around. I'm on I-495, southbound, but I haven't seen your exit yet."

"Okay, what have you passed so far?" I wonder if he used the directions that I emailed to him.

"I'm headed towards the Legion Bridge."

"Did you say the Legion Bridge?"

"Yes."

"Michael, you are not going south, you are going north and you are going in the wrong direction!" I exclaimed, losing my patience with him.

" Okay, let me take this next exit and go back the other way."

"Yes, you need to do that. Are you following the directions that I sent you?"

"Yes!"

If I didn't know any better, I would think he was getting an attitude with me because he can't follow directions. "Why are you yelling at me? I didn't get you lost!"

"Listen Raven, I don't want to argue. I'm now heading south. I should be at your place shortly. See you when I get there."

"Yeah, okay. Baby, be careful and don't forget that you will need to take the Baltimore-Washington Parkway towards Washington. Okay?"

"Okay baby, keep the bed warm 'cause I'm dog tired."

"Okay, see you soon. Love you."

"Ray, what did you just say?"

Oops! Slip of the tongue. "I said be safe," hoping the bad connection of his cell phone would help me fix that royal fuck up.

"Oh, okay, I will. See you soon, bye!"

"Bye." I held the phone, stunned and in total disbelief of the words that had just come out of my mouth. I can't possibly love him. I don't know him. I am meeting him, face to face, for the first time. Yes, we've talked day and night, consistently for a few months, but that doesn't mean love. Hell, we haven't even fucked yet. I can't fall in love with someone who hasn't even shown me what he can offer me sexually. Now I am tripping. Maybe him coming here wasn't such a good idea after all.

I finish getting myself fresh and clean for what I hope will be a night of good fornicating. Thirty minutes later, the doorbell rings. Slipping on my robe, I run to open the door. "Michael?" I hope this is the pizza delivery guy with the wrong unit. Standing in the doorway, not wanting to let him in, I am speechless. This brother can't be no more than five feet tall and two hundred-fifty pounds, at least. I am five-feet-two inches tall and can see clearly pass the top of his head. Maybe I could tell him that my plumbing is backed up or I just found out that my condo is rat infested and it would be best if he stayed in a hotel—stay anywhere—but just not with me! Now I can safely say that my 'love you' comment was definitely a slip of the tongue.

"Hi Ray, I made it!" He is just too damn excited for me.

"Yep, you sure did." I am trying to sound excited. "Come on in." Now I am beyond pissed and have reached pisstivity—is that a word? This brother waddles in my house with two suitcases, a suit bag and a duffel bag for three days? Naw, this turkey looks like he is prepared to stay for two weeks!

He leans in towards me, looking like Humpty Dumpty about to fall off of the fucking wall. "Can a brother get some love?" Without thinking, I wrap my arms around him and hug him tight, knowing in my heart that this is not going to be anything serious. He is just too short and plump for my taste and I could just kick myself.

"Wow Raven, you are more beautiful than your picture." He looks at me as if I am a fat, juicy T-bone steak that, in two seconds, will only be a bone. He looks hungry.

"And you don't look anything like your picture," I wanted to say, but couldn't. No matter how I'm feeling, I can't hurt his feelings. Folks can be very sensitive about their appearance. He really is a nice guy. If nothing more, we could be friends. "So, are you hungry? Care for a drink?" His eyes are making me feel totally naked and uncomfortable, even though I am wearing a terry cloth robe, tank top, flower-embossed boxer shorts and my favorite fuzzy slippers.

"No, not hungry, but I could use a drink. Hey, may I use your bathroom?"

"Sure, it's down the hall to your right and I will get started on our drinks." As he wobbles down the hall, I race to the kitchen phone to call Morgan. She is not going to believe this shit. This should put her concerns regarding my safety to rest. Morgan answered, sounding very irritated, as if I had just interrupted something that didn't want to be interrupted. Maybe her and Arthur were doing the nasty. After all, the phone did ring six times. "Morgan?"

"No, it's Mary Poppins! What do you want, Ray?"

"As always Morgan, kiss my ass."

"Yeah, well, I don't think Arthur has allotted me that much time off," she retorted with a giggle.

"He's here," I whispered, trying not to let my disappointment float down the hall to the bathroom.

Morgan has a rise of curiosity in her throat that has demolished the sarcasm. "Well, is he everything you expected?"

"He is everything I did not expect. Morgan, he looks like an egg."

"Well, at least you can have him for breakfast!" she exclaimed with laughter.

"Not in his wildest dreams."

"That's what you get for meeting men on the Internet." I can just picture her rolling on the floor with laughter as we speak. I feel like joining in on the fun, but I don't want Michael to hear me.

"Girl, not only is he short, he is also suffering from done-lapped disease."

"Done-lapped," she said, still laughing. "What the hell is that, Ray?"

"His stomach has passed his belt hoops and is bordering on the end of his zipper!"

She can barely get her words out from laughing at my dumb ass. "Well Ray, you know it's not what's on the outside, but what's on the inside that counts."

I can't say that I blame her for laughing at me, because I feel the same way. Except she is laughing and I feel like crying, because there will be no dick for me tonight. "Morgan, this man deceived me! As far as I am concerned, not only does he not have anything I want on the outside, I don't care for his inside either!"

"Well, what are you going to do, put him out?" She eased up on her laughter because she knows I will put him out on his ass. "Ray, he has traveled so far to see you. Can't you tolerate him for two days?"

"Nope. Gotta run. I can hear the toilet flushing. Bye." Michael opens the door too fast after the toilet flushes, which tells me that he did not wash his hands after playing with himself. Strike two.

After pouring our drinks, I sit on the sofa, watching this egg-shaped man look into my bedroom. If I didn't know any better, I would say that I just saw him digging in his ass! Not only is he short and fat, add nasty to the description. He has got to go.

"Ray, you've got a nice spot here."

He is so damn nosey. I try to keep the level of irritation in my voice to a bare minimum. "Thank you Michael, I appreciate that."

"No, I mean it. I really like your artwork. It's very black-like."

"Black-like?"

"Yeah, you know, sort of back to Africa décor." Michael is smiling and looking undesirable. Is that a gold tooth? Icky, I am not kissing him.

"I think the politically correct term is ethnic, not black-like."

Michael walks towards my floor-to-ceiling, wall-to-wall bookcase. "Yeah, that's it. That's what I meant to say." He's rubbing his fat little fingers over the spines of my books. "I see you read a lot of books too."

"Yep." I am glad he can read book spines, because he sucks at reading road directions. "So, Michael, do you have any hobbies?"

"I like to collect and refurbish old cars and sell them. And, a little this and a little that." He takes a sip of his drink and winks his eye at me.

"Meaning?"

He looks at me with those beady little eyes, with saliva trickling from the corners of his mouth. "Meaning, I love beautiful women, and right now, I am really digging on how beautiful you are," he salivated. Ignoring him, I walk to the kitchen to fix a plate of cheese and crackers, making a point to not put one switch in my hips, because I do not want to give this salivating egg any inclination that he is going to get any of me this weekend. If I don't eat while drinking this alcohol, this egg just might get fried tonight. "Ray, I noticed that you only have one bedroom," he yelled from the sofa where his behind was making a permanent indentation. "Where would you like for me to sleep?"

"That sofa pulls out into a full-sized bed and it's very comfortable."

Michael shows a hint of disappointment. "Okay, that will be fine."

I peeked around the corner. "What's wrong, you have a problem with sleeping on the sofa?"

"Well, no, not really."

"Are you sure?"

"I just figured that since we have been talking heavy for the past two months, that we were beyond sleeping on the sofa."

"Michael, despite what you may think or feel, the fact still remains that I don't know you. So therefore, you will sleep on the sofa. You should be happy that I have allowed you to park your feet under my damn table and rest your head on my pillow, instead of at a damn hotel," I said, with not a breath to spare. Whew, that sure felt good.

He raises his arms in the air as if I was a cop placing his ass under arrest. "Whoa, Raven. It really isn't that serious. I'm just saying that I thought we were closer than that."

"Well you thought wrong, 'cause it ain't happening here!" Looking into his pudgy face that has now drooped past his knees, I now feel like a jerk. "What a welcome, huh?"

"Yeah I've had better greetings, but it's okay."

I leaned against the wall with my arms folded across my chest. "No, it's not okay. I was wrong for my behavior and I apologize."

"Raven, it's okay, really." He walked towards me. "I was wrong for making assumptions about an arrangement that we never discussed." He clasped my hands with his. "I didn't mean to offend you, and you are right, you don't know me."

"We got off to a rocky start. Let's start over." Feeling the alcohol going to my head, I rush to the kitchen to get the plate of cheese and crackers.

After the cheese and crackers absorbed the alcohol from my brain, we decided to call it a night so that we could get a fresh start in the morning. Last week, Michael asked if we could hit a couple of clubs and do a bit of sightseeing. Tomorrow, I am going to keep him out all day and all night. This way, there won't be any temptation for him to ease into my bed, let alone anything else. Sorting through the linen closet for sheets for the sleep sofa, Michael yells as though he is on my balcony and I am down the street. "Ray, you have a great music collection. You weren't kidding when you said you were into old school!"

I grab the sheets from the closet, slam the door and march down the hall as if I was going to snatch a child right from where he stood. "Michael, why are you yelling? I am not deaf and my place is not that big." I feel like telling his ass to go stand in the corner.

"Oh, I'm sorry. I thought you were in the bathroom with the door closed."

"No, I wasn't. But, even if I were, you don't have to yell!" I feel myself getting heated, not because of the alcohol, thanks to the cheese and crackers, but because of his presence.

Sitting at the end of the sofa, thumbing through my CD collection and looking like a scolded puppy, Michael shakes his head. "Damn, this is just not my night, is it? I am fucking up all the way around."

"No, it's not and yes you are."

"Ray, is everything alright with you?"

"Yes, everything is just fine. I don't like to be yelled at, especially in my own house!"

"I think you are overreacting." He's looking at me as though I belong in a straight jacket.

"You think?"

He turned his back to me. "Yes, I do. It's not that heavy, or is it?" He shook his head and mumbled, "It must be that time of the month."

Oh no the fuck he didn't. I know damn well that this little stump did not just insult me in my house. Okay, that's strike three. Beat down time. "You know Michael, yes it is very heavy. I have a serious problem with you right now."

"I don't know why 'cause I did absolutely nothing to you." He is, obviously, feeling his oats as he slips in my *Best of Sade* CD and slightly turning up the volume, obviously to tune me out.

This little fat fuck has no clue. "Let's try deception for one, how about that?" I catapulted to the stereo system and pushed the OFF switch.

"I've been upfront with you for two months." He looks like a scared rabbit that's about to dash out of the door, never to return. "How did I deceive you, Ray?"

"You failed to tell me that you were short and fat, that's how! And, did I mention fat?" I tried to catch myself, but it was too late. "You made me say it. You made me tell you what I was feeling. It is all your fault."

Michael sat there, looking at me in total disbelief. Standing from where he sat, Michael walks over to me, takes my hand in his, intertwines my fingers with his, looks me in my eyes, rises up on his toes, and kisses my forehead. "I was hoping that you were mature enough to see past my physical flaws, Raven."

I wiggle my fingers free from his clammy paws. "And I am sorry that you weren't mature enough to be honest with me."

"I think I'd better leave. I am not feeling you right now." He is being very smug, as though he were having the last word.

"Yes, I think you should. Have a safe drive home." Those were my last words to Michael Anthony. "I am getting rid of that fucking computer tomorrow!" I yelled, slamming the door behind Humpty Dumpty.

5 / ramone's rapture (part 1)

Morgan called me at the crack of dawn, excited about some news she wanted to share with me. Since my weekend was shot to hell, thanks to Michael, I suggested we make a day of it and meet for lunch at the Terracotta Café, and afterwards, catch up on some shopping. Trying to pull myself out of bed on a Saturday has always been a hard task for me. Usually it's because I've spent most of Friday night into the wee hours of Saturday morning getting my brains fucked out. But today, I am bright-eyed and bushy-tailed. Before Michael arrived last night, Ramone had called and wanted to make his usual late night booty call, but I passed because I thought I was already gonna be dicked. Instead, I was emotionally drained from dealing with Michael's lame ass. I will have Ramone come over tonight.

Ramone and I have been going heavy for a couple of years. I still don't have his home phone number, nor do I know where he lives. If I need him for a tune up, I can page him or call him on his cell phone. So many nights I've wanted him to stay and wake up to him snuggled behind me and then bring him breakfast in bed. But, like clockwork, at two in the morning, he rolls out of my bed, into the shower and out the door. The motherfucker is probably married. Single as a one-dollar-bill my ass. I believe what is kept in the dark will come to light, eventually, which is why I am not losing any sleep over Ramone's ass. Besides, he's no Arthur. He can have five wives for all I care, as long as he keeps me maintained. I would be lying if I said I wouldn't be pissed if I found out the truth. I guess I could find out if I really wanted to know. I don't want to be bothered because, from the beginning, all Ramone has been to me is a booty call and he will remain that way until I get tired of his ass. And, right now, I need a tune up and he is the best mechanic in town. While dialing Ramone's cell phone number, I look through my closet to find something to get me in the mood.

"Hello," Ramone answered with a frog in his throat. After all, it is eight-thirty on a Saturday morning.

"Hey baby, got any plans this morning?"

He cleared his throat of the morning phlegm. "Naw, I ain't got no plans, why?"

"I want to see you."

"You will baby, tonight."

With my fingers crossed, I whined, "I know, but I was hoping that I could see you this morning too."

"Alright. Let me shower and get myself together."

Excited as hell 'cause I am going to get me some, I start exercising my Kegel muscles. "Okay! What time will you be here? I have to meet my sister this afternoon for lunch."

"Oh, well, is eleven good?"

"Perfect."

I am supposed to meet Morgan at one o'clock. I can call her and change the time, she won't mind. At least I don't think she would. Hell, I need this and her news will just have to wait an hour or two. Replacing the phone on the cradle, I sit on my bed and think of a good excuse to give Morgan. Then it hit me that I am a twenty-seven-year-old woman and I do not need to throw excuses to anyone, especially Morgan. Hell, I will just tell her the truth. I will tell her that I need to have my head banging against my headboard to make up for last night and that we will meet at three instead of one.

"Morgan, can we meet at three instead of one?" I pray she'd keep her whining to a minimum. Whenever Morgan doesn't get her way, she starts that damn whining.

"Dang Ray, why? I was looking forward to our lunch and I have something to tell you," she whined, just as I predicted.

"We will still have lunch, girl. But, instead of one, it will be at three. Okay?" Now I am pacifying a five-year-old child.

"Well, okay."

"Thanks Sis. Bye."

"Bye." Morgan sounded as though she was about to cry. I swear, she can be so damn dramatic, it's pitiful. Oh well, she'll get over it. I have an hour or so to get myself together.

6 / back down memory lane

I always have to prepare myself for Ramone's visits because I never know what he has up his sleeve. Ramone has a freaky side that I love. I made the mistake of telling Ramone about my fantasy of having a threesome with two men. Last month, Ramone and his buddy, Chas, showed up at my front door. Ramone said that they were in the area and thought they would stop by to say hello. After inviting them in, offering them a drink and having them make themselves at home, I pushed the OFF switch on my television and headed towards my sound system. I popped in The Whisper's *Greatest Hits* and then headed to the kitchen to prepare the drinks.

"Here we are." I placed the drinks on my brass, glass-topped coffee table that is adorned with gossip and décor magazines. Realizing that I forgot my coasters, I went back into the kitchen. "How about some snacks, guys?" I yelled over The Whisper's *Chocolate Girl*.

"Sounds good!" Ramone said.

Returning from the kitchen with a tray of hors' devours, I take my seat in the burgundy leather chair and plop my feet up on the matching ottoman, while Ramone and Chas made themselves comfortable, opposite me on the matching sofa.

"You have a nice place here Raven," Chas said, looking around at the clutter.

"Thank you." I knew he was being too nice because my place was a complete mess. Noticing the stained panties that were tossed in the corner last night from my moment with Ramone, I leapt from the chair to kick them out of view. "So, what brings you guys to my neck of the woods?"

Ramone and Chas mysteriously looked at each other, both grinning from ear to ear. "Well actually, we stopped by to see how we could take care of you," Chas said with a grin on his face.

Feeling totally confused and not very comfortable at the moment, I replied, "Excuse me?"

"Yeah," Ramone interjected. "Baby, remember last night when you told me of your threesome fantasy?"

Oh shit, he didn't! I can't believe he discussed my innermost thoughts with Chas—someone I don't know from a bunch of turnip greens. I took a sip of Remy Martin and tried to remain calm because I wanted to know what this was all about. "Yes, I remember. But Ramone, baby, that was something I shared with you and you only. I didn't expect for you to go and tell everyone you knew."

"Raven, don't be upset with Ramone. We were talking, you know, guy talk, and he mentioned that you were interested in doing a threesome," Chas said.

If looks could kill, there would be a chalk outline of Ramone's dead ass on the floor. Jumping to my feet, "I don't believe this shit!" I yelled. "Yall have got to go!"

Standing and almost tripping over my coffee table, "Raven, let's talk about this, baby," Ramone said.

"Be careful. I don't have money if you get hurt and try to sue me."

Ramone took my hand and led me towards the bedroom. "Chas, man, give us a minute." Ramone closed the bedroom door.

"Ramone, you have nothing to say to me. I can't believe you did that to me!"

"Baby, I want to help you."

"Help me? Oh, I see. You are helping me by putting all my business in the street, is that it?"

"No, baby. Please, listen to me..."

"Why don't I place a full-page ad in the *Daily Post* telling all the world that Ramone Jarvis enjoys having a finger shoved up his ass while fucking! How about that?" I yelled to the top of a whisper.

Ramone was obviously getting perturbed with me. "No, I wouldn't like that, Raven!"

"Well, what makes you think that I like the fact that you shared intimate details between you and me with your buddy *and* have the audacity to come to my place and talk about it to my fucking face!" As much as I tried, I couldn't hold back the tears of embarrassment. "That is so fucked up, Ramone! I can't believe you did that shit!"

Ramone caressed my face with the palms of his hands and gazed into my eyes. "Baby, I would never, ever do anything to hurt you. I care deeply for you, Raven, and you know this. I only want to make you happy and make sure that your mind and body are fulfilled." His lips gently touched mine. "I love you, don't you know that?"

Not knowing what to say, I stood there gazing into Ramone's beautiful hazel eyes, wanting him to take me and love me from the top of my head to the tips of my toes. I gathered my composure and forgot the fact that I was ready to kill his ass two seconds before his lips came into contact with mine. "Ramone, what is the purpose of your visit today?"

"To fulfill your fantasy." He kissed me, slipped his tongue in my mouth and palmed my breast. Damn, this man really knows how to make me moist.

I pulled away from his sweet embrace. "Ramone, I'm scared. I've never done this before. I don't know Chas that well."

"Baby, it's okay. It will be fine and Chas is good people. He's my boy and he is physically attracted to you and he wants to do this." Ramone unzipped my jeans, slipped his finger into my panties and rubbed my clit. "Baby, let me do this for you." Sighing and trembling, I nodded my head in agreement. "Good." He smiled and gently kissed me on my forehead. He removed his finger from me and tasted it. "Baby, you always taste so damn good." He turned and walked out of my bedroom.

"Ramone, wait! I don't know what to do. I've never done this before." I wanted to pinch myself to see if this shit was really happening.

"I will guide you. Trust me. You do trust me, don't you Ray?"

With barely an audible whisper, "Yes, I trust you."

Ramone left me standing there, not knowing which way to turn or if I should move at all. My panties were drenched from Ramone's touch. I dashed to my dresser and snatched out a clean pair of panties, then I ran into the bathroom to freshen up. I tried to mentally prepare myself for the adventure that I was about to embark upon, when I realized that it had been a few days since I trimmed by pubic hair. I like to keep that area free and clear of odor that could be trapped by the pubic hair, especially when it comes to oral sex. Ramone informed me that nobody wants a mouth full of pubic hair. I remember the first time he shaved me bald, he sucked areas of my pussy that I didn't know existed. Ramone knew exactly what he was talking about, but, I think the pussy is ugly and needs to be covered with hair. I opened the medicine cabinet and pulled out a new razor and proceeded to shave myself.

"Baby, are you alright?" Ramone pounded on the bathroom door as though the place was on fire, scared the fuck out of me and caused me to nick myself.

"Yes, I'm fine. I will be out in a minute. Please, give me a few minutes." I enforced the fact that I was getting ready for whatever was about to take place. Gathering my senses, I exited the bathroom and took, what seemed like a very long walk to the living room. Why did I feel like dead man walking? I really needed to get a grip. It wasn't that serious.

Chas was at the stereo, flipping through my collection of old school CDs and Ramone was sitting on the sofa, motioning for me to come and have a seat. "Hey Chas, man, why don't you pop in that Isley Brother's joint, *In Between the Sheets.*" Ramone gazed into my eyes. "Yeah, that's Ray's favorite and we need to make her feel comfortable." Chas found the CD and Ron Isley's voice floated throughout my condo, made me feel relaxed and put me in the mood for some freaky shit.

Ramone rose to his feet and stood in front of me. He guided my hands towards his sweat pants. I slid his pants down around his ankles. As usual, Ramone was free balling. This man does not like to wear underwear. He says it makes his nuts feel bunched up and they need to breathe. In my face, Ramone's dick was standing at attention. Was Chas standing there, staring and getting hot and bothered from seeing Ramone's hardness? I wondered if he was a fence straddler.

I stroked Ramone's ass, took him into my warm, moist mouth and sucked him like he was a tootsie pop and I desperately needed to find what was in the middle. I saw that Chas had unfastened his belt and unzipped his jeans. With his hands inside his pants, he began stroking himself, with his eyes plastered on what was taking place before him. Damn, he free balls too. Seeing that turned me on even more. I felt my juices flowing and my body temperature rising. Like the pro that I am, I removed Ramone from my mouth and turned towards Chas and motioned for him to joins us. I removed my shirt and bra to unveil the hardening of my nipples. Chas bent to his knees and took my nipple into his mouth. I positioned his dick in my right hand and began stroking him. Feeling Ramone's neglect, I grabbed his dick in my left hand. Stroking them, causing them to moan and groan with pleasure, I began to really feel this shit, and wanted to take the party to my bedroom.

My bedroom is the one place where I have complete control over the men who dare to enter, ceasing to become a place where I sleep, but a den of erotic pleasures. In the middle of this room is my bed where I laid, reclined on satin sheets that hold many secrets. I am naked, except for the silver bangles that adorn my wrists and rhinestones that sparkled from my earlobes; shimmering off of the Jasmine-scented flickering candlelight, making me feel more sexy and desirable.

Chas stood over me, nude. Every toned muscle in his body flexed, as he explored every inch of me with those beautiful, brown eyes, with eyelashes that reminded me of butterfly wings. I climbed on my knees, crawled my way to his erection, and then took him inside my mouth. Ramone was behind me, stroking me with his fingers, down to my asshole. He entered and exited my hole with his finger, as his soft lips gently planted kisses all over my round, firm butt. As Chas tickled my tonsils, I felt something wet and sticky roll from my back, down through the crack of my ass, and ooze into my opening. I didn't bother to turn to see what the icky feeling was, because I didn't want to stop the momentum that I'd built up with Chas. The look on Chas' face warned me that he was about to reach his climax. He grabbed the back of my head and stroked my mouth continuously. Ramone was sucking the sticky substance from my rear, as his finger mixed the substance with the juices in my honey pot. Feeling like I was ready to explode, I held back as intensity began to build, while Chas' body started to tremor, like he was experiencing a convulsion. "Oh damn!" Chas yelled, as he released his stream inside my mouth that trickled down the back of my throat. I didn't want to swallow his discharge, but I didn't have a choice. His hands continued to hold the back of my head, as he pushed himself down my throat, deeper and deeper. After his final thrust, Chas released his grip and wilted like a flower. I made a mental note to make myself vomit after they leave. Not allowing me time to breathe, let alone gather my composure, Ramone flipped me over like I was a rag doll and began to pound into me as though he was the jack hammer and I was the concrete he needed to break through. His body stiffened to the intensity of his climax which only took about two minutes to reach. He too, wilted like a flower.

Roles were changed in my bedroom that day, for I was not the dominant one. I had no control and I didn't even climax. This threesome shit ain't what folks make it out to be.

7 / ramone's rapture (part 2)

Preparing for Ramone, I hear a knock at my front door. Looking at my watch, I think that it is too early for Ramone, it's only ten o'clock. With my bra and panties on, I throw my robe around me and tighten the belt around my waist. Whoever is knocking is very persistent with a loud pounding on my door. I storm towards the door. "I'm coming, damn! You don't have to knock my fucking door down!" I yelled, flinging the door open to inhale the scent of Cool Water. Ramone stands in my path looking as though he was a Godsend.

"Hush ya fussin' girl. It ain't like you weren't expecting me."

"You're early."

Ramone looks good in a white short ensemble like he is on his way to the tennis court. "Yes, I know. I wanted to surprise you." Ramone has always been sexy from the bottom of his feet, all the way up to the only part that I am interested in.

"Well, don't just stand there, come on in."

"No, I like the view from right here." He loosened the belt from my waist.

"Huh?" I am dumbfounded as to what I am about to encounter, with The Ohio Players' *Sweet Sticky Thing* wafting from my bedroom to the front door. Ramone uses his index finger to ease apart the front opening of my robe. "Baby, can we bring this inside? I don't want the neighbors to know all of my business." Knowing he isn't going to succumb to my request, Ramone pulls me into him and parts my lips with his tongue, stroking them inside and out. Oh my goodness, here it comes. He is going to sex me right in the doorway! I am praying heavily that my neighbors stay inside their units until he is done. Knowing Ramone, this could take some time. Keeping my moaning to a slight audible whisper, he brings me in closer to feel his erection through his shorts, yearning for me to stroke him.

"Lay on the floor," he whispered in my ear.

His stare is making me feel helpless. "What?" I succumb to his demand.

Laying on my back, on the floor, in my doorway, for all to see, Ramone raises my legs, bends down and reaches for my panties. Kissing the inside of my thighs, he pulls off my panties. Pressing the palms of his hands against the bottoms of my feet, he bends my knees back towards my shoulders and instructs me to place my feet on the door trim. My legs are spread eagle, the width of the door's archway.

"Oh, Ramone. What in the…"

"Shhh," he said, covering my lips with his index finger.

I try to keep a steady heart rate as the brother in Unit 304 walks by to see me spread eagle in my doorway, looking like he wants to join in. While my eyes were focused on the brother from Unit 304, Ramone's lips are wrapped around my clit and sucking it like he was trying to get the last bit of juice from an orange. I can't hold back any longer and I don't care who hears me. I have got to get my ass out of this doorway, quick and fast before Old Lady Johnson comes out of her unit and has a heart attack at the sight of me having my pussy ravished by a crazed pussy lunatic. I grind my hips in unison with Ramone, to speed up the process. Helping myself along, I lick my index finger and roughly massage my nipples. Ramone, inserting two fingers inside me, begins to nibble on my clit, lifting the hood of my clit with his tongue to stroke underneath. With the intensity building, feeling the need to rush to the toilet, I let go of the buildup and cum in Ramone's mouth, as well as the hallway.

Ramone never fails to amaze me.

8 / sister to sister

Arriving fifteen minutes early at the Terracotta Café, I ask the hostess for a table for two in the non-smoking section. What other people do with or put in their bodies is their own business and nobody else's, but I'll be damned if I want to smell that shit while I'm eating. Getting myself acclimated with my accommodations, the waiter approaches my table with two glasses of water and silverware. "Not bad looking," I think to myself. Roaming his body with my eyes, obviously making him uncomfortable, I notice he has a nice bulge and big feet too.

"Will you be dining alone?" he asked, after sitting two glasses of water on the table and noticing two menus that sit in clear view. So much for smarts.

I moisten my lips with my tongue. "No, I am expecting my sister any minute."

"While you wait on your party, can I bring you a drink?"

I am looking at him with a smirk, being my usual flirtatious self. "Sure, I'll have a tall, dark and handsome, straight up."

He turned beet red. "How about a Coke instead?" No he didn't just blow me off. I look at him, smile and think that I don't want him any way. Besides, he looks like he needs to be in the damn circus with that big ass head. Hell, E.T. ain't got nothing on him.

Morgan approaches the table, laughing and making gestures towards me. "What the hell is so funny?"

"Damn Sis, that brother politely sat your ass on the curb!" Morgan laughs, sounding like a damn hyena.

"Kiss my ass, Morgan!"

"Whatever girl, you need to cut that shit out."

"Cut what shit out?"

"Do you ever take a break from trying to fuck every brother you see?"

"Bitch, don't hate me, 'cause you ain't me."

"I don't want to be like you, Whorina!"

"Whatever, hater!" We both fell out with laughter.

Perusing the menu, "Whew, girl I am starving!"

Morgan peeps over the top of her menu. "Humph, you should be starving."

"What is that supposed to mean?"

"You know exactly what I mean, Whorina."

Rolling my eyes, "I see you are talking out the side of your face again, as usual, Morgan."

"Whatever, Ray! All I know is that you put me on the back burner for a piece of dick!"

"Well, not really for a piece of dick."

"Yeah right. I know your ass better than you know it. Don't you realize that by now?"

"Well, Ramone did stop by this morning."

"Yeah, just as I figured. Tossed to the side for a piece of used up dick."

"Nope, see how much you know? He didn't stick me this time."

"You mean that horny toad just stopped by to shoot the shit?"

"Nope, and girl you will not believe the shit he did to me, whew!"

"What? I want to hear every detail, don't leave nothing out."

Just as I am about to fill Morgan in on my escapade with Ramone, E.T.'s brother returns for us to place our orders. "Are you ladies ready to order?" He is avoiding eye contact with me.

"Yes, we are. For an appetizer, I will have the Buffalo wings, extra spicy please, and for my entrée, I will have the Barbecue Ribs and Chicken Platter with Curly Fries and a side Caesar Salad please."

I watch her in astonishment. Who the hell is she ordering all of that damn food for, a damn army? Wondering if Morgan left enough for anyone else, I place my order. "I will have the Pasta Alfredo with Grilled Shrimp, please." I am trying to make eye contact with this brother, because I am determined to show him exactly what he passed up.

"Will there be anything else?" He is still avoiding eye contact with me.

"Yes, I'll have a diet Coke, please," Morgan chimed in.

Unbuttoning my blouse, "And, I would like something cold like a glass of Iced Tea; I'm feeling a little warm." I pulled my breast from my bra and exposed my hard nipples.

As he walks away in shock, Morgan is chopping on the bread that was placed on our table. "See, I told you that you were a nasty freak! He don't want you slut, get over it. Damn."

"Fuck you, Morgan."

"If you can't get the waiter to fuck you, what makes you think I would want to fuck your ass?"

"He must be gay."

"Either that or he knows a trick when he sees one," she laughed.

"Kiss my ass! Looks like I am not the only one hungry," I said, with just as much sarcasm as she dishes out to me. "Where in the hell are you going to put all of that food?"

Morgan ignores my question and directs me back to where we left off before we were interrupted. "Well, in a nutshell, Ramone knocked on my door, pulled my panties down, told me to lay on the floor in my doorway, spread eagle, while he went scuba diving for my ovaries."

"Raven, I don't believe that shit."

"Why do I have to lie?"

"Oh my damn! Girl, suppose one of your neighbors would have seen you with your ass up in the air like that?" Shaking her head in disgust, "Don't make no damn sense."

"Shit," I said with a chuckle in my throat. "They already did."

"What?"

"Yes indeed. The brother from Unit 304 came out of his unit and walked passed us, stopped in his tracks, turned around and made eye contact with me, while Ramone was between my legs." Morgan looks like she's just seen a ghost and I can't help but to laugh at the look of disbelief on her face. "I wish you could've seen the look on this brother's face!"

"Oh, see, that is so nasty!" She squinted up her nose like she smelled a dead skunk. "What did you do?"

"Hell, I laid there, gazed into the brother's eyes, continued to moan and groan, and really gave him a show."

"I know you did. You are such a trick."

"Girl, I grabbed the back of Ramone's head and commenced to fuck his face with my pussy."

"Damnnnnnnn! Shit, I have to change my panties with that one!" Morgan shook her head. "Hell, all I can do is live vicariously through you! Girl, that damn Ramone sure do some crazy shit to your ass. I guess you are the building sleaze now, huh?"

"Call me what you want, but that was some good shit and I would do it again in a minute!"

"I know your whorish ass would."

"Whatever, Miss Prissy Ass," I snarled. "Anyway, what's this news you need to share with me?"

"Oh girl, I almost forgot." She took a quick sip of her diet Coke. "I'm pregnant!"

"Huh? You what? Does Arthur know about this? No wonder you ordering half the fucking menu." I look at my sister with envy and wonder why it couldn't be me. "You're sitting over there glowing and shit."

"You heard me, and no he doesn't."

"Morgan, you know how he feels about you having babies. You know that having this baby could potentially jeopardize your life, right?"

"Ray, I am fine. My doctor is keeping a close eye on me and says that I should carry this baby to term with no complications."

"Mo, how far along are you?"

"Nine weeks."

"Nine weeks and you are just telling me, let alone not telling your husband?"

"Well, I didn't want to jinx it, and besides, I wanted to make sure that I was somewhat out of the woods before I told you or Arthur. I know how much having a son would mean to him and I didn't want you to get your hopes up, Auntie Raven."

"Yeah, and you also knew he would be against you having this baby, considering your current health."

"Get off of that Raven. You are not a doctor."

"Yeah, and I suppose you are?" Come on Morgan, I know how much being a mother means to you, but I want to keep you around for as long as I can."

She took my hands in hers. "Whorina, I am not going anywhere."

"Yeah, well, you better give me a niece so I can spoil her."

"You mean, so you can train her to be Whorina Junior?"

"Kiss my ass, Morgan!" I smiled at my big sister, hoping that she knows that I will be by her side through all of this.

"Hey, I want you to be the baby's Godmother. Will you?"

"Hell yeah, who else would it be?"

9 / close encounters of the married kind

It's been a long day. As I walk the three blocks from my office to my favorite watering hole, Roscoe's Restaurant and Bar, located on Vermont Avenue, I think to myself the reasons why I chose to practice urology instead of something easy, like pediatrics. Well actually, I should take that back. No physician's job is easy. People rely on us to save their lives and it's hard because physicians are human too. We aren't miracle workers, but we are aware of the science and technology out there to help people survive. Today, I had a patient whom I diagnosed, three months ago, with prostate cancer and it doesn't look good. By the time he made an appointment to see me, his cancer had metastasized from his prostate to other vital organs. This is very emotional for me. Seeing any of my patients terminally ill, and not being able to do anything to help them, other than to keep them comfortable and prescribe medication to ease the pain, is emotionally draining.

When I was nine years old, my father died of prostate cancer. Over a period of months, I watched my father suffer. Chemotherapy and radiation did nothing to help. I saw my father shrink from six-feet-two inches tall, two hundred fifty pounds to a mere weakling, weighing less than one hundred twenty pounds. Like most black men, he didn't have an annual check up or physical. So, at thirty-six years young, my father was laid to rest at Lincoln Cemetery. I know this sounds harsh, but I can't help being angry because a lot of what, we as black people bring on ourselves, can be prevented, simply by making an appointment; taking an hour out of our day to ensure we maintain good health.

As I approach Roscoe's, I see a familiar face. It looks like Malcolm Jeffries, a brother I attended high school with and later ended up being roommates with at Broward University. Damn, it's been almost twenty years since I've seen him. He has put on some weight. I wonder when was the last time he had a physical.

"Malcolm Jeffries!" I pulled him into an embrace.

"Well, I'll be damned, Arthur Carrington!"

"Yeah man, how have you been? It's been a long time."

"Man, I've been around. I've been going through some shit though. Me and my old lady aren't together anymore."

"Aw, I'm sorry to hear that."

"Naw, it's cool. How's Morgan?"

"Morgan is well, thanks for asking."

"Damn," is all I can say, standing there at a loss for words, searching the faces of people passing by, hoping that someone could read the expression of help on my face and give me an excuse to end this uncomfortable encounter.

At Broward University, Malcolm and I used to be tight. When you saw me, you saw him. He was my boy; close enough to be brothers, until I walked into our dorm room and found him ass up in some dude's face, getting his shit busted open. I packed my shit and found somewhere else to live. I wasn't about to live with no faggot. I like pussy and pussy only. I would've hated to break that fool up if he even thought about making a pass at me. Damn, that messed me up for a long time. I couldn't even look him in the face when our paths crossed on campus.

"Well, look man, I'm meeting a colleague and I'm already late." I hoped that he would get the hint.

"Oh, yeah, no problem. Listen, it was good seeing you. Give Morgan my love." He resumed the momentum in his step, as I hope to never see him again.

Taking the stairs that lead to Roscoe's, I am greeted by Shelly, the hostess, who escorts me to my usual spot in the back of the restaurant. Morgan must have phoned her and told her that I was coming. That's my baby, always got my back. "Evening Dr. C., your usual?" Shelly placed a black cocktail napkin with *Roscoe's* embossed in silver lettering on the table.

I take off my suit jacket and loosen my tie. "Hello Shelly, and yes, thank you."

"Fine. I will be right back with your drink." She turned on her heels and headed towards the bar, stopping to check on other patrons. Shelly works hard for her tips and she deserves them. She gives me nothing but first class service and I give her a first class tip.

Retrieving my brown leather cigar carrier, a Christmas gift from Morgan, from inside my suit jacket, I get the feeling that all eyes are on me. Shelly returns with my Hennessy, asking if there is anything else she can get for me. I tell her no, but I ask her to come back in ten minutes, because I would like to order dinner. "Will Morgan be joining you?"

"No, not this evening." Morgan insisted that I come to Roscoe's to relax and unwind. I can't help but feel as though someone is staring at me. Looking towards the bar, I catch a mirror eye contact with a lovely woman. She swivels on her bar stool, facing my direction, to make total eye contact with me. Picking up her drink, uncrossing her legs and dismounting the bar stool, she sashays in my direction. My eyes are fixated on the swing in her hips and I began to wonder what the motion was like in her ocean.

"Hi." She extended her right hand towards me. "Renee Jarvis, and you are?"

"Hi." I reached to shake her hand, "Arthur Carrington." She remained standing, and being the gentleman that my mother raised me to be, I stood up and pulled out the chair across from me. "Please, have a seat."

"Thank you. Do you come here often?" She peered into my eyes as if she could see straight through me.

"Yes, from time to time. You?" This woman is stunning. Her smooth chocolate complexion reminds me of a Hershey's Kiss. I just hope that there isn't a nut inside.

She parted her lips with her tongue. "No, this is my second time. My first time here was last week and I noticed you sitting here, in this same spot, alone."

Damn, she is hitting on me and I am flattered. "Oh, so you knew I would be here?"

"Let's just say that I was hoping," she smiled. "So, Arthur, what do you do?"

"Are you asking my profession?"

"Yes."

I take a sip of my Hennessy and think that this is going to be a pleasant evening. "I am a physician."

"Let me guess, OB/Gyn?" She giggled as if gynecology was a funny matter.

"No, urology."

"As in playing with penises?"

"Well, not exactly. I don't play with penises. I don't play with my profession. As a matter of fact, I take it very serious." Just as I figured, there's a nut inside.

"I didn't mean to offend you. Lighten up." She warmed my heart with her beautiful smile. With pretty white teeth and a chocolate complexion, I can only assume that this lady is far from the white blood that probably runs through her family from Masta.

"Sorry. It's been a long day."

"Tell me about it. I've been told that I am a good listener."

"No, maybe some other time."

"Yes, I would like to see you again." She is making me a little nervous.

"Is that a natural tan or did you not wear your wedding band?"

"Yes, I am married. Being a doctor, I am constantly washing my hands, so I tend not to wear my ring too often." Looking at her wedding finger, I notice a ring shadow as well. She must be on the prowl, since she removed her wedding ring.

"Are you married?"

"Yes." She answered without hesitation. Damn, I just knew she was going to lie.

I nodded my head towards her left hand. "Lost your ring?"

"No, I chose not to wear it tonight."

"Oh, I see. And how does your husband feel about that?"

"What my husband doesn't know won't hurt him. Now, will it?

"I don't know. I am not your husband." I took a sip of my drink. "Do you mind?" I removed my Romeo & Juliet cigar from its leather case.

"No, not at all. I love the smell of a cigar and a man who smokes one."

While taking in that last flirt, before I could light my cigar, my cell phone rings and I see from caller ID that it's Morgan calling me from the office. I excused myself from the table so that I could take the call in the men's room.

"Morgan, what's up baby?"

"Hi, honey. I'm closing up the office and I plan to take a cab home."

"No baby, a cab will cost you too much money. I can take you home."

"Nope, I won't hear of it, Arthur. You need to unwind. I will be fine."

"I don't feel comfortable with you hailing down a cab at this time of evening and having some stranger drive you all the way to Maryland, Morgan."

"Arthur, I will be just fine. Really."

"Where is Raven, can you call her and ask her to pick you up?"

"Yes Arthur, I can do that. Will that make you happy?"

"Yes, it will. Call me back and let me know if Ray is going to pick you up or not."

"Okay, Mr. Worry Wart, I will." Morgan blew a kiss into the receiver and ended the call.

Pressing the call-end button on my cell phone and placing it on the sink, I decide to take a leak before I leave the men's room. Washing my hands, I look into the mirror at a man that I don't recognize. What is wrong with me? I have a wonderful wife and I am about to have dinner with another woman. Sure, Morgan and I have gone through our ups and downs, but we have always come out strong and on top. This is wrong and I know it. That woman sitting out there had intrigued me. There is something about her and I want to get to know her better. While drying my hands with a paper towel, my cell phone rings. "Honey, not to worry. Ray is going to pick me up. She is on her way."

"Good, that's good. I don't mean to be a pain in the ass babe, but I do care about your safety."

"I know you do. I will see you at home."

"Right, baby. I won't be long. I am going to grab some dinner here and come straight home."

"No, don't rush. Take your time."

"Do you want me to bring you some dinner?"

"Nope. I will have Ray take me by Checkers. I'm feeling like a burger tonight."

"Okay, well, see you later."

"Bye honey, I love you!"

"I love you too."

Ending the call and exiting the bathroom, Morgan's words "I love you" haunt my mind as I walk towards another woman. I just can't do this. This isn't right. This is harmless. Its just dinner. Besides, Renee never indicated if she was going to have dinner with me or not.

"Welcome back."

"Thanks." With a nervous smile, I wonder how I am going to get out of this or if I even wanted to. Shelly walks over to ask if I am ready to order my dinner. "Would you care to join me?" I could just kick myself. Well, not really. Asking her to join me was the respectable thing to do.

"Sure, I would love to."

"Great. Shelly, I will have the Crab Cake Platter." I look towards Renee for her order.

"That sounds great, I'll have the same."

As Shelly walks away with our order, I think that I should be feeling very awkward, but I don't. I should be feeling guilty, but I don't. Instead, I am feeling like a teenager with his first piece of ass. Looking at her voluptuous bosom, I wonder if they are real.

"Arthur, I find myself very attracted to you."

"Ah, well…" Talk about being caught off guard.

"I realize this may be a little more than what you can swallow, but I feel that if I see something, or, shall I say, someone that I want, I go after him."

Right now, I feel like a pair of shoes that are on sale in Filo's Basement. "So, you saw me, and you are coming after me. Is that right?"

"My God Watson, I think he's got it!"

"Renee, I am flattered, really. But, I am a married man."

"And?"

"And I can't do this."

"Do what? We haven't done anything, yet."

"Well, you are a married woman."

"Tell me something I don't know, Arthur."

She gave me enough sarcasm to choke a cat, which tells me that she is not very happy with her marriage. This is probably why she is in bars picking up men, picking up me. "Do you always pick up men in bars?"

With no response, Renee stood up from her seat and stared down at me. "I don't pick up men, men pick me up!"

Well, I guess that is her way of telling me that I should be happy that she approached me, instead of the other way around. Although, I must admit, if she hadn't approached me, I probably would have changed my seat from the table to the bar stool beside her. "Renee, look, I'm sorry. Please, don't walk away angry."

Renee took her seat across from me with her head lowered. "No, I was wrong. You are a married man and your wife is very lucky to have you."

"Thank you. Will you stay and have dinner with me?"

"Yes, I would love too, but on one condition."

"Sure, what's that?"

"That we forget what just happened."

"It's a deal." I made room for Shelly to place our meals on the small table.

Renee and I talked for hours about our spouses, our likes, dislikes and our dreams. She is a housewife with two children—a girl and a boy—wanting to go back to school to finish her degree. I told her of my practice and about some of my patients, not revealing any names, of course. Mesmerized by her smile and laughter, I catch a glimpse of my watch and see that it is ten o'clock. "Oh my, we've been having such a wonderful and stimulating conversation, I have lost track of the time. It's getting late." I hate that this, whatever this is, has to end.

"Yes, I need to be getting home myself." She reached in her purse.

"Oh no, it's on me." I patted her hand, insisting that she put her money back in her purse.

"Thank you. The next one will be on me!"

"Sure, that sounds great!" I can't believe I just said that. Oh well, I've come this far. "Well, is there any way that I can contact you, Renee?"

"Sure, here is my cell phone number. Feel free to use it at any time."

"Just beautiful." I helped Renee with her wrap, tossed the twenty-dollar tip on the table and walked out arm and arm with my new friend.

10 / as the table turns

My desk clock flashes five-thirty and it is time for me to blow this chicken stand. I clean off my desk and prepare for my departure. I tell you, as far as I am concerned, being a secretary is for the fucking birds. "Raven, get me a cup of coffee. Raven, pick up my dry cleaning. Raven, pick up a birthday gift for my wife," is all I here all damn day. Since when did a secretary become a damn servant? Just as I am about to press the 'do not disturb' button on my telephone, Kathy, the receptionist, rings to inform me of an outside call that was on hold for me. "Who is it?" My damn day ended thirty minutes ago and she knew it.

"Charles Walker."

"Charles Walker?" Who in the hell is Charles Walker? Maybe this Walker guy is a bill collector. If so, he shouldn't be calling me on my job. I've told those assholes, time after time, not to call me at my place of business. Do they listen? Hell no, the bastards. They already ain't getting their money. If I lose my job because of them, they will never get their money.

"Yes, that's what I said. Charles Walker."

I know she is not forming an attitude with me. It's late, I'm tired, I'm not in the mood and I will go up to that front desk and smack that attitude right out of her face. I don't know why people insist on testing me. "Fine. Put him through." I am fixing my tongue to lash a gash right in this bill collector's feelings, calling me on my job.

"Hold on, I will connect the call."

"Raven Ward, may I help you?"

"Well, hello beautiful," came from this deep baritone voice that sent a chill from the top of my spine, down to the tip of my clit.

"Who's calling?" This can't possibly be a bill collector, not unless they have developed a new tactic.

"Hello Ray, its Charles." I still don't know who he is. But, he called me Ray and only people who personally know me, call me Ray.

"Charles? I am sorry, but I am not familiar with a Charles Walker. May I ask what this call is in reference to?"

"It's Chas, Ray. Chas is short for Charles. Sorry, I thought you knew." He's laughing and I haven't a clue as to what is so damn funny.

"Chas? Ramone's friend?"

"Yep, live and not on Memorex."

I don't find any of this funny, but I'm wondering why he is calling me. "What do I owe the pleasure of a call from you, Chas?"

"Well, you've been weighing pretty heavy on my mind and I thought it was time to tell you so."

"Oh?"

"Yes, ever since that afternoon we spent together at your place last month..."

"Oh, you mean that afternoon when Ramone, you and myself were together?"

"Yeah, ever since that day, I haven't been able to get you out of my head."

"I'm flattered. How did you get my work number?"

"This morning, I followed you from your home to your job..."

"Are you stalking me?" I am feeling very concerned.

"No, not at all."

"Then why did you follow me? Why didn't you just come and knock on my door like normal people do?" I think this guy might be a little off in the smarts department.

"I don't know. Bashful, I guess."

"Bashful? Chas, your ass is far from being bashful."

"Yes, true that. In all honesty, I just didn't know how to approach you."

"Chas, does Ramone know that you are calling me?"

"No, he doesn't. Does he need to know?"

"No, but you do know that Ramone and I are more than just friends, right?"

"You are? Besides screwing each other's brains out, what more do you have together?"

"Well, since you put it that way, I guess that is all that we have." Chas' question jerks me back into reality. "But what do you think he would say about his best friend calling the woman who he is, how you say, screwing the brains out of?" I am tempted to see what Chas has to offer, alone, and not with a third person involved. And, he is fine as shit too.

"Well, I would think that he couldn't say anything."

"What is that suppose to mean?"

"Look, you're single, right?"

"Last time I checked."

"Are you two committed to each other?"

"No, we aren't. But, he is the only one that I'm intimate with." I stepped to the side for fear of not wanting the lightening bolt that was about to strike my ass, to hit my computer.

"Huh?" Chas fell out with laughter. "Okay, please baby, don't take me for a fool. I know better than that."

"You don't know anything about me other than what you think you know."

"Okay, my bad. You're right. Let's squash this. Do you have any plans tonight?"

"Well, it is Friday and usually I do have plans, but you lucked up. What do you have in mind?"

"I thought that maybe you and I could hook up, get some dinner and get to know each other better."

"Sounds like a plan, except I'm really tired and don't feel much like going out to eat. You can come by my place, bring whatever you're drinking, and I will pick up something for us to eat. How about that?"

"Sounds good to me. But, I do know how Ramone likes to pop up at your place and surprise you from time to time. You think us being at your place is wise?"

"There you have it. It's my place and if Ramone shows up without calling, he will remain on the outside. So, how about Chinese?"

"Chinese sounds great. Nothing special, whatever you get will be fine."

"Great. I will see you, say, eight o'clock?"

"Okay, see you then."

"See you then." I started to hang up the phone, but decided to ask one more question. "Hey Chas?"

"Yeah?"

"You aren't married are you? I really don't want to get me or my feelings involved with a married man."

"No, I'm not married. But, why would that be a problem for you now?"

"Excuse me?" What in the hell is he talking about?

"Never mind, Ray. I will see you at eight o'clock."

I hesitate before I respond, thinking that maybe I don't want this man coming to my place after coming out his mouth like that. I'm tired and don't feel like no shit tonight. "Okay, see you at eight o'clock."

Hanging up the phone and pressing the 'do not disturb' button, I gather my belongings and head for the elevator. "Hold the elevator please!" I am running to make it to the elevator before the door closes. "Oh, Hi Jay." I am trying to catch my balance after leaping into the elevator.

"Hello Raven. Long time no see. How are you?"

"Yes. It has been quite some time, hasn't it?" I look at this gorgeous specimen and I can't help but reminisce on how we could never keep our hands off of each other.

Jay Dawson works in my building, on the twelfth floor. Jay and I were dating heavy about five years ago, and we almost made it to the altar. I was so in love with him, I couldn't see straight, not enough to see the damn truth. Not only was he fucking me, but he was also fucking Greta on the sixth floor, Angela on the tenth floor and Veronica on the first floor. This man carried this on for almost a year, and not one time within that year, did he get caught. He made sure his women never ran into each other, and that he scheduled us accordingly. He's a dog, but I've got to give the dog his due. The dog is good. Jay knew every inch of my body, and he loved oral sex so much, that he would taste my period from time to time. Every time I turned around, that man had my ass up in the air and didn't care where we were. Humph, now that I think about it, we had some good times in this elevator too.

"So Jay, how are you doing?"

"I'm doing fine, thanks. I can't complain."

Goodness, just the smell of this man makes me hot. Holding full eye contact, and desperately trying to control my breathing, I blurt out, "I've missed you."

"I've missed you too, Ray. I must admit, seeing you does bring back old memories."

Humph, he just doesn't know that he has just given me the license to start up some shit. "Well, let's do something about it."

"What are you talking about?" He should know me by now. I reach down and press the stop button on the elevator panel. "Ray, what are you doing?"

Looking into his eyes and dropping my belongings to the floor of the elevator, "Making up for lost time, baby."

I walked towards Jay, unloosened his tie and softly kissed his lips, using my tongue to part them. "Raven, we can't do this. This is not appropriate."

I bring myself closer, close enough to feel his hardening manhood against my pelvic bone. "Why Jay, are you committed?" I don't care what his response would be 'cause I'm a woman on a mission and I intend to see it through.

"No, no. I don't have a woman. But here, in the elevator?" He's not resisting me.

I begin to stroke his manhood. "It's never stopped us before, now has it?" I cut off his retort with my tongue.

Jay pulls me closer into him, grabbing and squeezing my breast and panting in my ear like a female dog in heat. "Ray, do you still believe in easy access?"

I placed his hand on my ass. "See for yourself."

Jay lifts my skirt and rips my pantyhose from my waist to thrust his finger inside my honey pot. Feeling my juices, he removes his finger, then inserts it into my mouth. "Here, taste how good you are." As I am sucking on his finger, Jay begins to get a little too rough. He turns me around, bends me over and instructs me not to bend my knees and to make sure that my palms are pressed flat on the elevator floor. He says he wants to see how limber I really am. Doing as he requested, Jay unzips my skirt and pulls it up over my head. Remaining in the instructed position, Jay pushes his hardness into me, stroking me with force. This position becoming uncomfortable, I slightly bend my knees. Jay smacks me on my ass as hard as he could. "I told you not to bend your fucking knees!" With a silent cry, I straighten my knees, grit down on my teeth and remain still and silent until he's done with his business. This is what I get for being so damn hot in the drawers. After two forceful thrusts, Jay ejaculates inside me. Afterwards, he asked if I was on the pill. Tears of anger and humiliation stream down my face. "Too late for that shit now, don't you think?"

Without a word, Jay gathers his bearings and his belongings, push the start button on the elevator panel, stare me down with disgust in his eyes and then exit on Level B1. Fortunately, my car is parked on Level B2. Now I can walk to my car and cry in silence.

11 / what's done in the dark shall come to light

Driving out of the building garage, while trying to gather my composure, I call Morgan. I knew that she wasn't home, but just hearing her voice on her answering machine would make me feel safe and secure.

"You have reached the Carrington's residence. No one is available to take your call. Please leave your name, number and a brief message and someone will return your call. Thank you and have a blessed day."

Trying my best to keep my cry silent, "Mo, this is Ray. I didn't want anything, just calling to check on you. Call me."

I lost control of the situation. Jay and I dated for five years, and he knows me too well. That bastard turned the tables on me. And, for the first time, I didn't know how to take it. I felt weak and helpless, and I don't like feeling that way. I will get his ass back for that shit. Mark my words, I am not finished with his ass yet.

Approaching the Main Street exit, the aroma of hot steamed crabs entice me to make a stop at the Southwest Waterfront, also known as the Wharf. Instead of Chinese, I'll pick up a dozen of steamed crabs, a pound of shrimp and a flounder to stuff with crabmeat. I hope Chas is not allergic to shellfish. Oh well, if he is, then it's more for me. Feeling more relaxed after my horrific experience with Jay, I park my car in front of the fish boats and lower the top on my red '99 Mustang convertible. Grabbing my purse, I exit the car and begin perusing what the different fish boats had to offer. For the most part, all of the prices are the same and they all claim to be fresh. But, I am quite sure they don't have freezers in the rear of their boats just for the hell of it. After making my purchases, before I head home, I make a beeline to the grocery store; I need to pick up a douche, I feel nasty.

Arriving in front of my condo, I walk by the brother from Unit 304 getting into his car and raping me with his beady little eyes. "Why don't you take a picture, it will last longer?"

"If I had my camera on me a few weeks ago, I would have done just that!"

Giving him the middle finger, I proceed to my mailbox to retrieve my mail, then continue up three flights of stairs to my unit. Damn, why couldn't I have purchased a condo in a building with an elevator? Purchasing that Stairmaster was a waste of money. I need to send that shit back and get my damn money refunded. Tossing my purse and jacket on the sofa, I begin to sort through my mail. An envelope addressed from the condo's homeowners' association catches my attention. Walking towards my stereo system, pressing the ON switch and popping in Peabo's *Feel the Fire*, I make a seat for myself on the sofa and open the envelope from the association.

24 August

Ms. Raven Ward

West House Condominium, Unit 300

Re: Violation of Condominium Association Rules and Regulations

Dear Ms. Ward:

The West House Condominium Association (the "Association") would like to inform you of the dissatisfaction with the illegal sexual conduct that took place a few weeks ago, within the confines of the public hallway, outside of your unit.

We have received several complaints that you and your house guest have chosen to involve the entire building in your sexual misconduct, thereby, holding you in violation of your signed agreement.

Ms. Ward, what you do inside of your unit is your private business. However, when it overflows into the public access areas of the building, it becomes the business of the Association.

The Association has taken this act into effect as your first violation. Therefore, we will not file any charges and will allow this letter to be your first and only warning.

In the future, we would appreciate you showing your neighbors the same respect that they show you and keep your business inside of your unit.

Sincerely,

Amaretta Snead-Jackson

President, West House Condominium Association

Laughing to myself, I toss the letter aside, thinking that I will definitely have to frame this one. Seeing that I have an hour to get myself ready for Chas, I prepare the stuffed flounder and toss it into the oven to bake on three hundred and fifty degrees. Pulling off my clothing, leaving a trail, I make a beeline straight to the shower. After my encounter with Jay, I feel quite tainted.

Reaching for my scrub brush and increasing the water temperature to be as hot as I can stand it, I vigorously scrub myself, trying to scrub off the layer of skin where Jay defiled me with his clammy hands. "That bastard."

Winding down my shower, I reach for my towel. Wrapping it around me, I leave a wet trail of footprints from the bathroom, leading to the bedroom, flop on my bed and wrap myself in my week-old satin sheets. "Time to change these bad boys," I said aloud. After drying myself off with my sheets, I pull out a pair of gray sweat pants and a T-shirt. I decide to leave the panties and bra where they lay, in my top dresser drawer. I don't feel like being confined tonight. Easy access is what I always say. Walking to the kitchen to check on the stuffed flounder, I hear a knock at the door. Thinking its Chas, I open the door without asking who was there. With a smile on my face that instantly turned to confusion and disappointment, there stood Ramone. "Hey baby, you don't look too happy to see me."

"Of course I'm happy to see you. What are you doing here?"

"I didn't have any plans, so I thought I would stop by."

The LCD clock on my stereo system flashes six forty-five. I hope Chas operates on CP time. I've got to think of something really fast before he gets here.

"Oh, well, I have plans. As a matter of fact, I was in the middle of getting dressed," I wasn't lying, but I was hoping that would do the trick.

"Oh, where you headed?"

"Um, Morgan is having a gathering at her place tonight."

"Well, Morgan lives pretty far. You coming back home tonight?"

"Um, nope, not at all. I will be staying there. I don't want to make that drive back tonight." I am about to piss on myself from being nervous at the thought that Chas could walk up those steps any minute.

"Oh, I see. Damn, baby girl, what you cooking in there? Hey, you aren't going to ask me in?"

Getting antsy and shifting my weight from side to side, "Baby, listen, I've got to hurry up and get out of here. Its stuffed flounder that I'm taking to Morgan's gathering."

"Alright, well I won't hold you." After fondling my breast and giving me his usual, make my panties wet, kiss on the lips, he turns and starts walking down the hall. "Call me tomorrow."

"Sure, baby." I closed the door and ran to the kitchen to grab a paper bag. I feel like I'm about to hyperventilate. A few minutes later, a knock at the door startles me. I run to the window to make sure that Ramone's car is gone before I open the door. "Just a minute," I called out, trying to gather my composure. Ramone's unexpected visit doesn't sit right with me at all. "Hi Chas, right on time. Come on in. Have a seat," I offered, pointing to the sofa.

"Hey Ray, are you all right, you look a little jumpy?"

"Yes, I'm fine." I don't know if I can trust Chas enough to tell him why I was about to jump out of my skin.

"You sure?"

I form a phony smile on my face. "Yes, I'm sure."

Chas looks at me like he didn't believe a word I said. "Okay, well I picked up a bottle of wine. Something sure does smell good. I don't remember Chinese food smelling this good. You cooked?"

"Yeah, I couldn't resist. The crabs smelled so good coming from the Wharf, so we are having crabs, spiced shrimp and flounder stuffed with crab. I hope you like seafood."

"Damn girl, you don't mess around! What black folk in D.C. do you know that don't like seafood, especially crabs? When do we eat?"

"Well, let me check on the stuffed flounder and set up the table."

"Mind if I help?"

Shocked to have someone, especially a man, offer to help do anything other than remove my clothes, "Sure. Could you pull out some wine glasses for me? They are in the third cabinet from the refrigerator." I can't help but think how nice it is to have a man, in my kitchen, helping me.

"Sure. So, how are things?" He's opening the wrong cabinet. Just like a man, he opens two cabinets before he opens the one I told him to open.

"Things are just fine." He stares me down, because he knows that I am lying through my teeth. "Chas, I try very hard not to wear my emotions on my sleeve. When something is bothering me, I prefer to work it out on my own."

"Well, I've been told that I am a good listener."

"Listen Chas, let's just have a nice evening, okay?"

Taking me in his arms, "Absolutely. But, I want you to know that you can talk to me about anything. I will not judge you, Ray. All I want to do is make sure that you are happy and I don't want you to worry your pretty little head over something that can be eliminated just by talking about it."

"You know, don't you?"

"That Ramone showed up out of the blue?"

"Yes, but how?"

"As I was pulling into your complex, I saw him coming out of your building. I laid low so he wouldn't see me. I waited ten minutes before I came in, just in case he decided to double back."

"I didn't think I was going to be able to get rid of his ass and all I could think about was you two bumping into each other. I felt so uncomfortable. The way he was acting and asking so many damn questions, it's like he knew something was up," I opened the oven to check the stuffed flounder. "Almost done."

"If it will make you feel comfortable, we can hang out at my place from now on."

Of all the men that I have dated, not one has ever invited me to their home. "Your place?"

"Sure. I live alone. Of course, I live like a bachelor, so I would have to clean up."

"I bet you do. I can see the shit-stained drawers lining the floor now."

"Damn, I don't think I'm that bad."

"Oh, I almost forgot, I have to make my crab sauce." I opened the refrigerator and grabbed the needed ingredients.

"Let me guess, mayo, ketchup, vinegar and hot sauce, right?"

"Yes, how did you know?" I give him a love tap on his arm.

"Everyone I know makes that stuff to dip the crab meat in."

"Hell, its some good shit. Ghetto, but good!"

"Oh shit!" Chas knocked over the bottle of wine with his arm from laughing so hard.

I reached for the dishtowel to wipe up the spill. "Don't worry about it."

"No, please let me clean that up. After all, I was the jackass who knocked it over."

"Oh please, Chas. It was an accident."

"Yeah, but I only purchased one bottle."

"Hmm, yes, well that is a problem, isn't it?" I pondered. "In the same cabinet where you got the wine glasses, pull out two brandy snifters. You do drink brandy, don't you?"

"Sure do. Point me in the right direction." He flashed that Colgate smile and gave me a kiss on the cheek.

"In the living room, on the mini bar cart. Oh, and while you are out there, put on something more upbeat. I feel like groovin' tonight. Let's have some go-go up in this joint!"

"Go-Go? Sure thing baby girl. Who do you have?"

"Chuck Brown, Rare Essence, EU, TCB, shit, I even got some Junk Yard up in this camp!"

"Awww shit, let me find out!" he yelled. "You are my kind of girl."

Chas popped in Chuck Brown's *Run Joe* and returned to the kitchen with the brandy and poured us each a glass. "So," he said, making eye contact with me and bobbing his head to the beat of the congas.

"So." I am feeling myself really digging this guy and shaking my ass.

"What about the crabs?" He begins to sing lyrics from the song. Actually, he is yelling 'cause he can't sing worth a damn.

"I hear ya now, but Chuck Brown you ain't!" I chuckled. "Now, do me a favor and run your ass to the hall closet and pull out some newspaper and spread it on the dining room table, please."

"Sure. Shall I put some on the floor too?"

"What for?"

"To catch the shells and stuff from the crabs."

"No indeed, that's what the vacuum is for." Removing the stuffed flounder from the oven, "Dinner's ready!" I sang, as Chas comes into the kitchen to give me a hand. "Yo Chuck, grab the mallets from the drawer, please."

Chas grabs the mallet and takes a seat at the dining room table. "Whatever man. Looks good."

I grab a crab from the top of the pile in the middle of the table and yank the legs from the poor thing. "Well, I hope it tastes as good as it looks!"

"I am sure you will."

For once, I am speechless. All I can do is blush. Damn, he is saying and doing all of the right things. Now I know how Morgan feels. "Chas, earlier, when I asked you if you were married, because I didn't want to be involved with a married man, you asked why should it make a difference now. Where did that come from?"

"Ignorance, I guess. I didn't mean anything by it. Actually, I was out of line and I apologize."

"No need to apologize, but I'm sure that there is a reason why you said it and I doubt if it had anything to do with ignorance."

"Ray, it's really not my place. What you do is your business and so is who you do it with."

Knowing that he knew something that I didn't know, but I obviously, needed to know, "I see. Chas, do you have something you would like to tell me?"

"I really don't want to get in the middle of you and Ramone. Ramone is my boy and it's bad enough I'm sitting here enjoying myself with his woman behind his back."

"Okay, I am not Ramone's woman. I am my own woman and I will see who I choose to see."

"Really? If that were the case, why did you lie to Ramone to get him to leave, instead of telling him the truth that you had a date?"

"Who said I lied to him?"

"Did you tell him that you had plans with someone else tonight?"

"Well, no."

"Well, you didn't tell him the truth."

"Well, I sort of told him the truth. I told him that I had plans tonight, but with my sister."

"Thank you for making my point."

"You have a point?"

"My point is that there is much more to you and Ramone, if you can't tell him that you are dating other people."

"But, this is not a date."

"What is this if it's not a date, Ray?"

"Well, two friends getting together for crabs."

"Maybe for you it is. For me, it's a date. I am very attracted to you Ray, and although I know of your past, I want to see if I can make an honest woman of you."

"Honest woman? Oh, now see, you are about to cross that line Chas, and believe me, you don't want to go there with me." I feel myself getting pissed.

"That didn't come out right."

"You're right, it sure didn't!"

"Let's move on to another topic, okay?"

"No, it's not okay. I like to finish what I start."

"Ray, I didn't come here to argue with you. You are a beautiful, desirable woman. You are flawless. You make every bone in my body ache. I have been craving you for so long. Hell, woman, I wanted you before that shit went down last month. I wanted you so bad that when Ramone approached me about having the threesome, I agreed because I wanted so badly to feel you and you to feel me. Do you think that I really wanted to have my shit rock hard with another motherfucker in the room? Hell no." Chas got up from the table, walked over to the window and peered out at the view.

"Chas, why did you wait until now to tell me all of this?"

"I told you, I didn't know how to approach you. This morning, I got up the nerve to drive over here to your place. Just as I was about to get out of my car, you were coming out of your building, walking towards your car. I guess I lost my nerve. But, the drive from your place to your job helped me to find my nerve. Then you disappeared into the garage. I went into the lobby and asked the Concierge if he knew Raven Ward and he told me what company you worked for. He offered to call up to your office, but I declined. Again, losing my nerve. There is just something about you that makes me weak when I am near you. Anyway, it wasn't until five o'clock that I got up the nerve to call you. I called and hung up five times, before I went through with the call. You are an intimidating woman, Raven. You are always in control, and well, I wasn't sure if I was your type of man. After all, I am definitely not Ramone. Thank goodness."

Getting up from my seat at the table, I walk towards him. "What do you mean you are not Ramone?"

"I am different, Raven. I don't treat women like a piece of ass. I treat women like the queens that they are. I would never show up at your door and take you in the hallway for all the world to see." Chas verbally smacked me and it stung.

"You know about that?"

"Yes. I know about every sexual encounter. Ramone can't hold water. But, I see he doesn't tell what he doesn't want you to know."

"Look at me, Chas." I placed my hand on his shoulder and turned him towards me.

"Ray, I love you. I've always loved you." He held his head down like he was about to be sent to the corner.

I lift his chin with my hand. "Chas, I need to ask you something, before we go any further, and I need you to be totally honest with me."

"Ray, will you be able to handle my honesty? I don't want you to be hurt."

"Yes, as long as you are here with me, I believe I can handle anything." I took a deep sigh and looked into his eyes, trying to hold back the tears. "Chas, Ramone is married, isn't he?"

"Yeah, and with kids." He turned his back towards me, not wanting to see the hurt in my eyes.

I feel as though someone had just stabbed me in the back with a dull knife. "I guess I've always known or felt it, but never wanted to face it."

"Well, if you always knew or felt that he was married, why would you continue to see him?"

"Because he makes me feel good. Ramone is dependable and he doesn't come with any hang-ups or strings attached. He always seemed to call or come around at the right time, except for tonight," I chuckled, attempting to lighten the mood.

"I'm sorry Ray, I didn't want to hurt you. But, I don't want to see you mistreated."

"Oh baby, don't worry about me. Ramone has not mistreated me. Anything that Ramone has lied to me about, I allowed it to happen. I have control over my destiny. And, well, I knew that some day, Ramone and I would end. I just didn't know when."

"So, are you ending it with Ramone?"

"It depends."

"Depends on what?"

"On you."

12 / why cry over spilled milk?

Tomorrow is my boss' wife's birthday, and just like last year, and the year before, he forgot to buy her a gift. And, just like last year and the year before, he threw a one-hundred-dollar bill at me and told me to pick her up something nice. And, just like last year, and the year before, I picked up something that costed twenty dollars or less and pocketed the rest. Hell, it ain't like he knows the difference. Shit, my services cost money, exactly eighty dollars. Besides, I get to take the afternoon off so that I can find the perfect gift. So, just like last year, and the year before, I will stop by the thrift store on my way home, to see what I can find. His wife likes to collect antiques, and I am always finding her nice antique-like vases or artwork at the thrift store, for twenty dollars or less. You can find some really nice things in the thrift store, if you take the time to look. Now, I don't buy any clothes from there, because I don't believe in wearing clothes from people I don't know. They may have had the cooties or something. I should feel guilty about taking his money, but I don't. I look at it this way, you pay for what you get. He needs to be doing this shit himself. Hell, I ain't the one fucking her. Word around the office is that he ain't the one fucking her either. I am always booking vacations for his wife; at least five times a year and he never goes with her. Now, I can understand spouses needing to take separate vacations to make time for themselves and whatnot, but five vacations in one year? Alone? That shit smells fishy to me, and my boss is so damn dumb, he can't see the forest for the damn trees.

My desk clock strikes noon and it is time for me to blow this joint for the day. As I am gathering my belongings, Marcy Douglas walks by my desk, looking like she's just lost her best friend. "Marcy, is everything okay?"

"Yes, everything is fine." Tears begins to stream down her cheeks.

I pass her the box of tissues from my desk. "Hold up, girl. Why are you crying?"

"I'm sorry. I just, I just…"

"It's okay. Umm, you want to talk?"

"No, I don't want to bore you with the details."

"It's no problem. Let me grab my things and we can go down to my car and talk, okay?"

"I don't want to put you out, Raven."

"Don't be silly. I'm leaving for the day and I'm on my own time, with plenty to spare. Let's go."

Escorting Marcy to the elevator, I extend the tissue box to her, wanting her to get herself together before we reach the lobby where there is constant traffic and, not to mention, one nosey ass receptionist. Damn, I can't stand that hussy. She reports everything she sees and hears to the boss. I suppose she is gathering brownie points or something. But after four years of kissing the boss' ass, you would think she would be away from that front desk by now or maybe not. Maybe she should try opening her legs, instead of telling everyone's business. Pushing the down button to call the elevator, I reminisce on my experience with Jay. Every dog has his or her day. Walking to my car and putting my things in the trunk, I offer Marcy a piece of gum to calm her down. She declined. "Marcy, nothing can be that bad sweetie, to make you lose control like this, can it?" I unlock the passenger door for Marcy.

"Raven, I don't understand what I did wrong."

"Wrong about what? Does this have to do with work?"

"No, it doesn't."

"Well Marcy, what's wrong?" Hoping to get a response, but to no avail. I know she isn't married, but what the hell, folks don't need to be married to have a baby anymore. "Marcy, are you pregnant?"

"No, I'm not pregnant."

"Are you sick?"

"No, I'm not sick."

Getting just a little irritated with her ass, because right now, I could be riding to the thrift store with my top down and my music cranking. "Well, excuse me Marcy, but would you mind telling me what the fuck is wrong with you? I am not going to waste my time playing Go Fish with your ass."

"Raven, I'm sorry. But, I don't know how to say it."

"Say what?"

With a long deep sigh, Marcy lets me have it. "My lover dumped me."

"You mean you are crying over dick?"

"No, she…"

"She?"

"Means the world to me."

"Marcy, are you a lesbian?"

"No, I am not a lesbian."

"Well, what do you call it? You are bumping pussies with another woman. By my definition and just about everyone else's in the universe, you are a lesbian."

"I wasn't when I met her. I mean, when I met Cassie, I had just broken up with Jay, who left me because he couldn't handle the pressures of being in an interracial relationship."

I try to keep the look of disgust from my face. "Interracial relationship? You mean you were dating a brother?" I don't see what black men see in white women, especially this one sitting in front of me. She is truly showing her weakness.

"Yes. Does that bother you?"

"Well, let's just say that I have my opinions regarding interracial relationships, just as I have opinions about everything else under the sun. But, we aren't discussing my opinions right now. Why did things end between you and Cassie?"

"Cassie felt that I wasn't totally over Jay."

"Were you?"

"I thought I was. I mean, I could've been over him, easily. But I can't seem to get over how our relationship ended."

"If you don't mind me asking, how did it end?"

"How much time do you have?"

"I have some time." I look at my watch and think that this is going to be a long one. "How about you? What time does your lunch end?"

"My boss is on travel all week, so I can take as much time as I need."

"Good. Let's go for a ride. I will bring you back."

"Okay, I could use some air. Can we put the top down?"

"Hell yeah, girl!" I flipped the switch to drop the top.

Pulling out of the garage and then turning down K Street, I make my way to Haines Point. I figure it would be a great place for us to sit and talk and Marcy can get everything off of her chest. Turning on the radio, I suggest to Marcy that we just enjoy the ride and listen to a bit of jazz until we get to our destination. We arrive at Haines Point, I decide to park where you can see the planes take off and land at National Airport. "You want to walk around or just sit here?"

"No, sitting here will be just fine."

"Good." I pull a rolled joint from my purse. "You smoke?"

"Yeah, from time to time."

"Oh, in other words, you smoke other folks' shit."

"Yep!"

"Well, this will help calm your nerves. This is good shit too." I light the joint, then inhale deeply. After two or three tokes, I offer the joint to Marcy.

"So Marcy, school a sista, 'cause I don't know. What's it like being with a woman? I mean, since you aren't a lesbian and all, what made you turn to a woman?"

"Well, let me take you from the beginning. That way, you can get a better understanding of my relationship with Cassie." She passes me the joint.

"Okay, you have my full attention." I turn off the radio, recline my seat and take a few more tokes.

"Well, Jay and I had been dating for three years. For the most part, our relationship was perfect. We were planning to be married; at least that is what I thought. We were inseparable and we never paid any attention to what people thought or said. Besides, our families didn't seem to have a problem with our relationship, so we didn't care. As long as we were together and we loved each other, that was all that mattered. However, his friends were a different story all together. They had a big problem with me. I guess because they gave him such a hard time when he would bring me around, he stopped. We even stopped going out in public. Everything stopped, except for the sex, until I caught him with another woman."

I was curious to know this 'Jay' person's last name, because it sounds like some shit that Jay Dawson would do. "Oh, damn, I bet that must've really fucked you up to catch Jay, whatever his name is, with some trick bitch, huh?"

"Yes, it did, very much. I guess it wouldn't have hurt so much if I hadn't caught him and that bitch fucking in my bed. I could never forgive Jay Dawson for humiliating me!" She started up that damn crying again.

I reach for the box of tissues that I had tossed in the back seat and hand her another tissue. "How did you catch this Jay Dawson and this bitch in your bed together?" I feel so sorry for her. "Men, I swear, if they didn't have what I liked so much between their legs, I wouldn't fuck with them either.

Don't quite know if I would turn to pussy though." Jay Dawson, huh? Oh this is too easy.

Blowing her nose, "I left work early because I wasn't feeling well and I noticed his car was in the parking lot. It was my place, but he had a key. Anyway, as I opened the door, an unfamiliar scent smacked me in my face, a woman's fragrance; very strong. I could smell the sex in the air and not to mention, I saw her funky stained drawers in the middle of the floor. I heard moaning and groaning coming from the bedroom. I didn't have to hesitate, I knew exactly what was going on. I went into the kitchen, grabbed a knife from my cutlery set and walked towards the bedroom. Before opening the door, I stood there and I listened for a long time. I heard her calling out my man's name. I heard him calling her 'baby' and telling her that he loved her. I couldn't take it anymore, so I flung the door open and lunged at him. I was aiming for his dick. I threw her clothes out the window, so she had to leave out of my apartment butt naked and he followed her."

"Damn! I don't blame you for ending it. Did you seek revenge on his ass?"

"No. I didn't seek revenge, but I thought about it. I contemplated doing a lot of things to ruin his life, but I figured that his life wasn't worth it. So, I blocked the thought out of my head."

"So, when did Cassie come into the picture?"

"When I went to her house to talk to her about fucking my man in my bed."

"Huh?" I said, looking confused as hell.

"Yes, Cassie was the woman that was fucking my man!"

"Is Cassie black or white?"

"She's a beautiful black woman."

"With a name like Cassie?" I chuckled to myself.

"Well, last time I checked, pussy ain't got no face and dick ain't got no conscience, so I doubt if they have names attached to them too."

"Damn, well, you right about that! But, I don't understand. Why would you get involved with the same woman you caught fucking your man in your house?"

"When I went to see Cassie, she was very apologetic and she explained to me that she didn't know that Jay was involved with me. As a matter of fact, he had told her that he was single and had a female roommate. I believed she was telling me the truth. I began to cry and one thing led to another. And before I knew it, Cassie was pleasing me between my legs."

"Damn, that's some freaky shit."

"Yeah, well…"

"Hell, didn't she question him about having a so-called female roommate? I know I would have."

"Yes. He told her that his roommate was a white woman and that he didn't fuck trash."

"Marcy, listen girlfriend, you don't cry over dick or pussy, especially when there is an over-abundance. Now, let's stop this pity party, get yourself together and move on. Marcy, you are not the one at fault here and you have got to get that through your head. You need to realize that you, and only you, have control over your being and no one else does. So, if you cry, you cry because of you, not because of someone else. Hell, girl you should be the one to turn the fucking table, not have the table turned on you. It is Cassie's fault that you are sitting here crying your heart out. She is the one who you found fucking your man in your bed. It is Jay's fault that you are here crying because he wasn't man enough to stand up to his boys, or anyone else for that matter, who objected to his relationship with you. And furthermore, he is weak as shit for even using that as an excuse to go fuck someone else! Got it?"

"Yes, I got it and you are right. Ray, I don't know how to thank you. I really needed someone to talk to and I appreciate you being here."

"Don't be silly. It's no big deal at all."

"Well, I appreciate you."

"Thank you, Marcy. Listen, you have any plans this weekend?"

"No, why?"

"Good, you need to get out! Let's take in a movie this weekend. How about Saturday night?"

"Sure, I would love too."

"Great! Now, we better get you back to the office before they send out a search party for your ass!" We filled the car with laughter, music and another joint.

13 / thinking with the wrong head

It's been a week since my encounter with Renee and I think it's true what they say about men thinking with the head in their pants instead of the head on their shoulders. That has to be the case for me. I cannot seem to keep my mind off Renee. I am almost sure that has everything to do with the rise in my pants when I think about her round, voluptuous rump swaying from side to side, and those round, perky breasts. Renee does not have anything that Morgan does not have. So, why am I so intrigued? That night at Roscoe's, I felt just like I was on my first high school date. I sat across from her with a rock hard dick. I was fidgety and giddy just like a teenager, except the only thing I was missing was a bad case of acne. Hell, if Morgan had not called me when she did, I probably would have released in my pants. This is wrong and I know it, which is why I cannot bring myself to dial her number. After all, I am a married man. Even married men have female acquaintances. Regardless, I love my wife and I know that this is wrong. Not to mention adultery is against the law. If Morgan found out about Renee and me, she would file for divorce and take me for every dime that I have, including my practice. Raven would probably see to it that my face is plastered all over the Six O'clock News, as well as in every newspaper in the Washington metropolitan area. Once her crazy ass sister gets involved, I can just hang it up. Hell, I could see the headlines now, *"A Prominent D.C. Urologist found faced down in the gutter with a .22 caliber slug enlarged in the back of his head."* That damn Raven will do serious harm to anyone who brings pain to Morgan. Those two are thick as thieves.

One time, Morgan and I had a disagreement, and well, I put my hands on her. I did not strike her, I shoved her. Nevertheless, that was still the wrong thing to do. I should have just walked away. However, walking away is hard to do when it comes to Morgan, because she will not let you. Morgan called Raven crying, and before she could hang up the telephone, Raven was walking through my front door with her .22 aimed at my head. She would have pulled the trigger, if Morgan had not pleaded with her. I will never forget the look in Raven's eyes, pure hatred. Now, I would rather cut off my hand than to strike Morgan. Besides, I want my life! I am no fool. Hell, this time she would probably cut my body up, hide bits and pieces of me around

Washington, D.C., and send the authorities on a body hunt. I don't put shit past Raven Ward. She is vindictive and just as mean as a fucking snake. I don't ever recall seeing a sensitive side to Ray. I have never seen her shed tears, nothing. I am glad Morgan is just the opposite. Morgan has a lot of mouth and is very argumentative, but when it comes to physical altercations, Morgan has Raven to fight her battles.

"Honey," Morgan called over the intercom system, breaking my train of thought.

"Yes?"

"John Howard is on the line. He wants to know if you can cover him tonight at the hospital."

"Sure, unless you have something planned for us."

"Hmm, well, what I have planned for us can wait until you get home." Morgan can be such a flirt.

"Well then, I'll make it a point to end the rounds as early as I can."

"Okay baby, so should I tell him that you will do it?"

"Yes, thank you."

Without giving additional thought, I pick up the telephone to dial Renee's cell telephone number.

It sounds as though I may have awakened her. "Hello."

"This is Dr. Carrington calling for Renee Jarvis." I tried to sound professional.

"Well, well, well. I didn't think I would hear from you, Arthur. How are you?"

"I am fine, thanks. And yourself?

"I know you are fine baby, but how are you?"

"I am doing well," I said, chuckling and enjoying her flirting.

"Good to hear. So, what took you so long to call me?"

"Cold feet, I suppose."

"Well, I don't bite, baby."

"No, I know you don't. Listen Renee, I am not very good at this…"

"I bet you are good at everything you set your mind to." Renee threw off my concentration with her sexual semantics.

"You know, I'm sorry. I should not have called you because this is so wrong. I am not interested in having an affair behind my wife's back. This is way too much for me to handle right now."

"No, wait! Arthur, I'm sorry. I realize I can come on a little too strong. I am making you feel uncomfortable and I don't want you to feel that way. How about we meet for dinner and talk?"

"I don't think that would be a good idea, Renee. I am no good at this. I don't know how to be with another woman. I don't know how to cheat. I can't be intimate with you and then lay in bed next to my wife at night. I just can't do it." I sound like a big old pussy.

"Arthur, we don't have to be intimate. I enjoy your company and your conversation very much. I would love to see you again, just to talk. If nothing more, we could become friends."

"Yes, well I don't see anything wrong with being friends."

With excitement in her voice, "No, there isn't. So, when are we going to get together?"

"Well, let me check my schedule and get back with you, alright?" I asked, knowing damn well that I will regret all of what I am about to get myself into.

"Sure! I will look forward to hearing your voice again," she said, hanging up her cell phone.

Well, you've really gone and done it now Arthur. You have started up something that will be hard as shit to end. Shoot, maybe I am getting myself worked up over nothing. Dinner with a friend is harmless. After all, I have dinner with female colleagues all the time. Although, being around my female colleagues don't give me a hard dick either.

"Arthur?" came from the intercom.

"Yes, Morgan."

"John Howard is on line one for you, again."

"Great, I'll take it. Thank you baby."

"You're welcome."

Releasing the intercom button and pressing line one, "Dr. Howard?"

"That's me!" he exclaimed with laughter. It never amazes me how the slightest little thing can tickle this man.

"How are you John? It's been a while."

"Art, I can't complain. You ready to get your ass whipped on the course Saturday?"

"Man, please! In your dreams, what time?"

"It will have to be early. I have a Cystoscopy at nine in the morning. How about five-thirty?"

"In the morning? On a Saturday?" I am usually knee deep inside of Morgan at that time of morning.

"Yeah, sorry. That's the only time I can hit the greens, unless you want to switch to another day."

"Can't. My schedule is tight for the next two weeks. The ass-crack of dawn it will have to be. I will call and schedule."

"Excellent. Oh, I almost forgot why I was calling. I want to thank you for covering me tonight…"

"No problem. You've covered my ass a number of times."

"I know, but it's not necessary now. I thought I had a conflict with my scheduling, but my secretary straightened things out for me. So, I will be able to do my rounds tonight."

"No problem. Well, I am here if you need me the next time."

"I appreciate that Art. It's nice to know that I can count on you. Now, go get some rest. You're going to need it for the ass whipping you will receive on Saturday!"

"Yeah, we will see! Take care man." I dialed Renee's phone number.

"Well, that was quick."

"How did you know it was me?" I should have blocked my office number. There I go again, thinking with the wrong head.

"I have caller ID, just like the rest of the world."

"Oh, I see. Well Renee, this is my office number, my wife is my office manager and she periodically answers the phone…"

"Not to worry, Arthur. I won't call you at the office, okay?"

"Okay." I make a mental note to never call her from home and to always use my cell phone from now on.

"So, when is dinner?"

"Tonight, eight o'clock at the Seafood Club on K Street."

"Sounds good. I will be there with bells on."

"Please wear more than bells. This place does enforce a dress code."

14 / its hardly over

It's Friday night, I'm bored out of my mind and horny as hell. Since Chas filled me in on Ramone's dirty little secret, I refuse to call him. Come to think of it, I haven't heard from Ramone either. But, it's only been a week and it's not unusual for me to go that long without hearing from him. His wife probably has him on lockdown. Ramone has always said that I had the best pussy he's ever felt or tasted, so I will be hearing from him soon. But, the question is, do I want to hear from him? Hell no, once a liar, always a liar. I remember my mother saying that a leopard don't change its' spots, just rearranges them. Fuck Ramone Jarvis and feed his ass a fish head, that adulterous bastard. I hope he gets the cooties or something.

This week, Chas has shown me what its like to be treated like a lady and not like some dime store whore. First of all, he doesn't show up at my door without calling, and when he does show up, fucking me into a coma is not on his agenda. Well, at least it hasn't been this week. It's still new and he is probably still feeling me out. Two days in a row, he has sent flowers to my job with beautiful cards attached. The other day, I found a small box of chocolates on the windshield of my car, along with a note telling me how glad he was that he and I were becoming a couple. I thought that was so sweet, but a little assuming on his part. He didn't discuss being a couple with me, or how I even felt about it. Chas is real smart too. He can hold an intelligent conversation about anything under the sun. He knows a lot of miscellaneous shit too, like, why the sky is blue and about some place called the lights points or point of lights or some shit I ain't never heard of in my life. And, when it comes to black history, the brother is sharp as a tack. Hell, even I didn't know that a black man invented ice cream. We are a smart people and it's too bad the kids of today don't realize that. Chas calls me every morning to make sure I am up and to wish me a wonderful day. Now, that's real special treatment. He ain't offered to pay no bills up in this joint. Hell, this pussy ain't free, but he ain't hit it yet either. As a matter of fact, he hasn't even tried to hit it. What's he waiting for? Hell, it ain't like I haven't been making passes at him, and it's not like I don't want to. All I know is that I really do like Chas and I kind of sort of want to see what this could be and where this could go.

Morgan is constantly telling me that I need to slow my ass down and find someone of my own. Believe me, I've been searching for an Arthur, but I've had no luck. Shit, if they could clone his ass, I would be the first in line. He is a good man though, treats Morgan with much respect. Well, he does now, after I had to show him that I would put a bullet in his head. But, come to think of it, that was only one time and prior to that incident, he had never put his hands on her. They were going through some really tough times in their marriage and I know how Morgan can be. She always has to have the last word. That girl will gnaw at you until she breaks you down and even I, at times, feel like slapping the shit out of her. But instead, I tell her to kiss my ass. It helps to relieve the urge of swiping the back of my hand across her face. So, I am sure that Morgan had pushed that man to his limits. Hell, I keep telling her everyone has a limit and can only be pushed but so far. Well, it finally came to a head. She had pushed and pushed and he turned around and shoved her into a wall. He didn't cause her any physical damage, just mentally, because he shocked the fuck out of her. So, of course, she calls me, and well, while I know her ass was dead wrong, I had to come to her defense. But, I love my brother-in-law and I always will.

I sure hope I hear from Chas tonight. I am feeling lonely, horny and I want to try to get me some dick tonight, shit. I called him, left a message telling him to call me on my cell phone, because I would probably be surfing the Internet when he called. I refuse to get a second phone line; I believe Eastern Bell is getting enough of my damn money as it is. While on the Internet, I receive an instant message from an unfamiliar screen name.

ItsHardlyOver:	Hello.
RavenWard27:	Hi.
ItsHardlyOver:	How have you been?
RavenWard27:	I've been great. Who is this?
ItsHardlyOver:	That's good. I've been trying to get over the fucked up shit you did to me.
RavenWard27:	I haven't done shit to you. I don't fucking know you.
ItsHardlyOver:	Oh, you know me.
RavenWard27:	Okay, I give. Who are you?

ItsHardlyOver: Guess.

RavenWard27:   Guess? Okay, mirror, mirror on the fucking wall, who is
                   this wacko motherfucker in my fucking IMs?

ItsHardlyOver: Oh, that's real funny. I didn't know bitches had a sense of
                   humor.

RavenWard27:   \<sigh\>

ItsHardlyOver: Okay, I will give you a hint.

RavenWard27:   Thank you.

ItsHardlyOver: I failed to tell you that I was short and fat. Oh, and did I
                   mention short and fat?

RavenWard27:   Michael Anthony?

ItsHardlyOver: Well, it isn't true what they say about bitches, you do have
                   a brain.

RavenWard27:   I ain't gonna be too many bitches for you, fat boy.

ItsHardlyOver: Yes Raven, this is Michael. Short, fat and in your face.

RavenWard27:   Michael, I've been meaning to call you. I really feel bad
                   about how I treated you. I was wrong and I am sorry.

ItsHardlyOver: Sure you are, Raven.

RavenWard27:   No, I am. I was wrong for what I did. But, you did deceive
                   me by sending me a fake pic.

ItsHardlyOver: No BITCH, I didn't deceive you! I loved you and you
                   disregarded my feelings. You are the fake ass BITCH!

RavenWard27:   You fat little fucker. You will never, ever get a smell of this
                   pussy, do you hear me? So, I suggest you do not IM me
                   ever again. Lose some fucking wait and work on your self-
                   esteem, you fucking egg!

ItsHardlyOver: The correct spelling is WEIGHT, you dumb whore.

RavenWard27:   Kiss my ass. And, you need to lose some of that too!

ItsHardlyOver: Check out the name, Raven the Bitch...trust me,
                   ItsHardlyOver!

RavenWard27:   No, you trust me, Michael. You don't want to fuck with
                   me. You need to ask around, Raven Ward is not the one to
                   be fucked with. Not now, not ever. I will make your life
                   pure hell. I suggest you recognize that and recognize it real
                   quick! Now, do me a favor and kiss the crack of my ass.

And, if you EVER contact me again. Now, have a nice fucking day, you tub of lard.

ItsHardlyOver: Ooh, I'm shaking.

RavenWard27:   Fudge packer!

Turning off my computer, I search for Michael's cell phone number because I am going to call that little fat fucker and give him a big ass piece of my mind. How dare him and who does he think he is? That little fat fucker is probably married too! That's why I only have a cell phone and a pager number for his ass, instead of a fucking home number. "Damn Raven, you are smarter than that! Stop fucking with these assholes who don't turn over a home phone number!" I yelled aloud.

While tearing up my desk, looking for fat Michael's phone number, my phone rings. I hope like hell it is him, the wannabe skinny bastard. Without checking caller ID, I snatch the phone from the cradle. "Hello!"

"Ray?" Chas' voice has a calming affect on my nerves.

I took a deep sigh. "Hi baby."

"What's wrong?"

"Nothing."

"Why did you answer the phone like that?"

"No reason. Just a little stressed, I guess. It's been a long day."

"Oh, well how about letting me take you away from that stress tonight?"

"Sure, what do you have in mind?"

"A friend told me about this seafood restaurant on K Street. You hungry?"

"Yeah, I could use a bite to eat."

"Great, I will pick you up in an hour, okay?"

"Okay baby, see you then. Bye."

Wanting to release the tension knots that fatso had put on my shoulders, I decide to soak in a relaxing bath for a minute. While testing the temperature of the bath water, I see that I am badly in need of a pedicure. Nobody in their right mind would want to suck on these paint-chipped toes. Reaching for the nail polish remover and a few cotton balls, my phone rings, startling me and causing me to drop the bottle of nail polish remover into the tub of water. "Shit!" I reach for the phone without checking caller ID.

"You will pay for what you did Raven," the threatening voice said.

"Michael, fuck you and your whole fucking fat family!" I slammed the cordless phone into its cradle. "Damn, some people just can't take rejection.

Get over it!" I walk to the kitchen, pour myself a tall glass of wine to enjoy with my bath. Walking towards the bathroom, I detour into my bedroom to retrieve a joint from the shoe box that I keep on the top shelf of my closet. As usual, I need to use the ottoman to stand on to reach the top of the closet. Once immersed in the warm bath, I light my joint, sip my wine and get myself in the mood for Chas. Thinking about Chas isn't working. I need my rock, I need Morgan.

"Doctor's office," came from the voice on the other end.

"Morgan Carrington, please."

"Sure. May I tell Morgan who's calling?"

"Yes, this is Raven."

"Hi Raven, this is Stephanie."

"Hey Stephanie, how are you?"

"Girl, I can't complain. You know a sista got her hair did. When you gon' come and check it out? Don't wait too long, it won't last past a few days."

"I'll get down there one day soon."

"Yeah, you do that. Okay, hold on and I'll get Morgan for you. But, be careful, she must be on the rag or something."

"Okay, thanks!"

"No problem sista." She placed me on hold.

"Hey Ray, what's up?"

"Not much. I just needed to hear your voice."

"What's wrong?"

"Girl, I just had a run in with Michael Anthony."

"What do you mean?"

"Girl, I was on the Internet and that jerk IM'ed me."

"IM'ed you? What's that?"

"He instant messaged me, you Internet illiterate hoe!"

"Go to hell, Ray. I thought you said you had blocked him from doing that?"

"I did, but he created a new screen name. It's like he's stalking me or something."

"Well, just block this screen name and every other screen name he IM's you with. Or, change your screen name."

"Yeah, I think I will do that. But girl, he called me too. He basically threatened me, Mo. He told me that what I did to him was fucked up and that it wasn't over yet, whatever that means."

"Well Ray, I've told you about treating people like they are less than you and not respecting other people's feelings. That man drove from Cleveland to D.C. to see you, and believe me, that is not a short trip. You were wrong for the way you handled it, but I'm not saying that him calling you and threatening you was right, either."

"Damn Morgan, whose fucking side are you on? I mean, damn, that asshole got me all freaked out and I call you to get support and you side with him? I don't believe this shit."

"Ray, I am only telling it like I see it. If you can't handle the truth, then you'd better learn how. You know I don't hold any cut cards with you. You were wrong girl, plain and simple. He probably just wanted to scare you, and he succeeded. I told you about bringing men from the Internet to your house," she scolded. "Anyway, change your phone number or block his number. If he persists with the phone calls, call the police and file a report."

"I don't think he will call again, but it's just eerie. I've never had anyone to do this to me before."

"Feels funny when the shoe is on the other foot, huh?"

"Mo, am I that bad?"

"Baby girl, yes."

"Well, I don't mean to hurt people's feelings, but I just believe in being honest. You are the one who has always told me that honesty is the best policy, right?"

"Yes, except for when you have a lack of concern for people's feelings. Ray, I believe, from personal experience, that people will take better to your criticism of them, if you are giving it with love and respect."

"Morgan, that man deceived me, he lied to me. I am to show love and respect to someone like that?"

"Yes."

"What about do unto others as you would have them do unto you?"

"Is that what you want from Michael? For him to do unto you as you have done unto him? Because if that is what you want, looks like you've already gotten it."

"I get your point, Mo."

"Good. Feel better?"

"Yep!" I said, not feeling any better.

I am more upset than I was when I dialed the damn number. I was expecting Morgan to side with me, not with Thumper. For once, I would like for Morgan to side with me, whether I am wrong or right. But deep inside, I know that will not happen, because that is how Morgan lives her life, by being honest and tactful.

"So, it's Friday night, I know you've got plans. Where are you going?"

"Chas is taking me to that new seafood restaurant on K Street for dinner. He's picking me up at eight o'clock. We have reservations for eight-thirty."

"Yeah, I've heard of that place, Seafood Club or something like that. Well, you've got fifteen minutes and I know you aren't ready, are you? You are probably sitting your behind in that damn bath tub."

"How did you know?"

"Because whenever you feel threatened or hurt, you have two safe havens—me and that damn bath tub. See, I told you I know you better than you know yourself."

"Yep, I suppose you do. What time is it?"

"Seven forty-five. Get out of that tub and be on time for a change. I hear that the Seafood Club is very nice and classy. They have a dress code. So, wear something pretty."

"I was going to throw on a pair of jeans."

"No, don't do that. From what I hear, they will turn your ass around at the door for wearing jeans. Wear a cute pant suit or a dress."

"A dress? Morgan, I'm not going to church, I'm going to eat!"

"Okay, wear a casual suit, you tomboy!"

"Whatever. Why are you still at the office this late?"

"Well, I've got a lot of work to do. We are having our books audited and I need to make sure that they are in shape for the auditors. Arthur is covering for John Howard for a few hours at the hospital tonight, so he will pick me up afterwards."

"Okay, well, be careful. I don't like you down there by yourself at night."

"Not to worry, Stephanie is hanging out with me and we will take her home."

"Good. Well, let me throw on my clothes and I will call you in the morning."

"Okay, I'll be looking forward to it. Have fun and don't do anything I wouldn't do."

"Girl, I am planning to do what you would do, what you wouldn't do and things you wouldn't think about doing!"

"Eww, you are so nasty! And you want to know why I named you Whorina!"

"Love ya. I'll talk to you tomorrow, bye!" I placed the phone on the cradle and pull myself out of the, now chilled, bath water.

Spraying cologne behind my ears and other unmentionable areas, I take Morgan's advice and slip on my linen jumper with the same flat sandals I wore when I met Ramone, the rat bastard.

Grabbing my purse and a lightweight sweater, I decide to meet Chas downstairs. For once, I am on time and anxious to see my man.

15 / too close for comfort

Sitting in the foyer of the Seafood Club, trying to convince myself that it's just dinner with a friend, I play with the change in my pocket, while waiting for Renee. Just like a woman, she's ten minutes late, and with each passing minute, I lose an inch of my nerves. If she doesn't get here within the next five minutes, all of my nerve-building will go down the drain and I will run like hell.

I should be waiting for my wife, not another woman. I can't do this to Morgan and I won't. I am stronger than this. I made a vow before God to be faithful to her and I am going to stick to that vow. Instead of tonight being a beginning for Renee, it will be the end. I can't see her anymore. Being friends is out of the question as well. I just hope that she is not one of those stalker-type women.

"Hi Arthur, sorry I'm late. I had to drop the kids off at the babysitter's house."

"Oh? What about your husband, he couldn't watch them?"

"No. He is out tonight, just like he is every other night. He probably has some bitch on the side."

"You think so?" The hostess escorts us to our table. I requested to be seated in the back where it is dimly lit. I couldn't chance being placed in the open and get noticed by someone who knows me or Morgan.

"Yes, I think so. Ramone is never home. When his cell phone rings or pager goes off, he is out the damn door. I am not a stupid woman. He must be fucking someone else, because he sure ain't fucking me."

"Oh, I see. Maybe it's not another woman. Maybe he is an undercover drug dealer or something." Where have I heard the name Ramone before?

"Drug dealer?" she chuckled. "Well, if he is selling drugs, I sure as hell don't see any of the profits."

"Well, let's change the topic. We want to enjoy ourselves, not make ourselves depressed."

"Sounds good to me. I'd rather focus on you anyway."

"Renee, I thought we had already discussed that we would just be friends. Your sexual innuendoes are making me very uncomfortable and I would like for them to stop."

"Okay, I'll stop, for now," she said, smiling, locking her eyes with mine. This woman just doesn't quit.

"Hello and welcome to the Seafood Club. My name is Monica and I will be your server for the evening. Is this your first visit?"

"Yes, it is. I've heard a lot of wonderful things about your establishment."

"That's good. The best marketing is word of mouth. Would you care to start off with a cocktail?"

"Yes, I would like a brandy, straight up, please." I look towards Renee.

"Monica, I'll have a Chardonnay, please."

"Great, I'll be back with your cocktails. In the meantime, this evening's specials are listed on the back of the menu. Each day, these specials are suggested by the Chef. The Flounder with Blue Crab Stuffing is delicious."

"Hmm, that does sound yummy. I love crab. I think I will try that dish!" Renee said.

"Great, I will be back in a few minutes to take your orders." Monica walked away, stopping to check on other patrons.

Perusing the three-paged menu, "I think I'll have the Lobster. It's been a while since I've had a good Lobster. They have so much to choose from."

"Arthur?"

"Yes."

"Thank you."

"For?"

"For showing me a wonderful evening."

"The evening is just getting started. You may hate me at the end." Renee probably won't feel that this evening is so wonderful after I tell her that I can't see her anymore.

"Nonsense. How could I hate you. How could I hate anyone who brought me to such a nice place. The only place Ramone takes me is the Mom & Pop's Chicken Shack on Florida Avenue. Hell, Ramone's idea of a good time is a pack of hot dogs and movie rentals."

"Well, that doesn't sound like too much fun to me."

"It isn't."

"Renee, how long have you been married?"

"A very long ten years."

"That's a long time. Are you not happy?"

"No, I'm not."

"Is that why you are here with me, because you aren't happy with your husband?"

"It could be. The first few years of my marriage were marital bliss. I couldn't have been happier. Damn, the things that man did to me in our bed were indescribable and, I must say, embarrassing. Ramone is very uninhibited when it comes to sexuality. He believes in living out your fantasies and we've lived out every fantasy that I've ever dreamed of," she said with a sigh. "But, somewhere along the way, he lost interest in me."

"But you are a very beautiful woman. How could he lose interest in you?"

"I don't know. I ask myself that every day. I guess, just like with ice cream, if you have too much of the same flavor, you choose another."

"I am sorry to hear that, Renee."

"Don't be sorry, Arthur. It's not your fault. It's my fault for staying in a marriage that I know is not right for me. But, I have two kids and I have to hang in there for their sakes. I don't want my kids growing up without a daddy. But, as soon as they finish high school, and hopefully go to college, I will leave."

"You have it all planned out, don't you?"

"I don't know. I just don't know."

"So, you really think he is having an affair?"

"Like I told you earlier, if he isn't fucking me, he must be fucking someone else. Besides, it wouldn't be the first time."

"What do you mean?"

Monica approaches with our drinks. "Here you are. Are you ready to order?" She places our drinks on a white cocktail napkin along with a basket of hot rolls on the table.

"Yes, I will have the Flounder with Blue Crab Stuffing," Renee ordered.

"And I'll have the Lobster. But first, I would like to have Fried Calamari as the appetizer."

"Great. Miss, would you care for an appetizer before your meal?"

"No thanks. I will have a taste of his Fried Calamari."

"Okay, thanks. I will return shortly with your appetizer."

"Arthur, two years ago, I found out that my husband was having an affair."

"How did you find out?"

"Well, typically I don't bother with the bills. I leave that to Ramone. Well, I made some charges on our credit card and when the bill came in, I wanted to see the grand total so that I could give him the money when he paid the bill. On that bill was a charge for a hotel room. That was not one of the charges that I made. I contacted the credit card company, got the name and number to the hotel and made the call. The representative told me that Mr. and Mrs. Jarvis were guests in their establishment for two days and that they had signed room service receipts, as well as credit card receipts to prove the legitimacy of the charges."

"Damn, the hotel gave you that much information? I didn't think they could do that?"

"Well, I don't think that they are suppose to divulge that type of information. I told them that I was Mrs. Jarvis and that I did not recall staying at their hotel, and if they could not show me any proof, that I was going to sue their asses for credit card fraud."

"Wow!" I am definitely going to end this. This woman is scorned, and if she is this resourceful, I know that Morgan can be even more resourceful, especially with that damn Raven helping her out.

"Wow, indeed. Once you mention lawsuit, you can get whatever you want out of folks. Don't you realize that this society is built on lawsuits? Hell, I should've been a damn lawyer!"

"So, how did you approach him?"

"Well, I haven't said anything yet. I kept tabs on his comings and goings and the times that his cell phone would ring or his pager would buzz. I kept a log of everything. So one night, I decided that I would hang out with a girlfriend, at least that is what he thought. Instead, I dropped my kids off at the babysitter's house and I sat in my car, one block away from where I had his car in clear view. When he left, I followed him."

"He didn't notice that you were following him?"

"Hell no. When Ramone drives, he is too busy blasting his music and talking on that damn cell phone. Besides, I made sure to stay at least two car lengths behind him and it was dark. All he could see was the headlights of my car. Anyway, just as I clocked his ass, at ten o'clock he left the house, got in his car and I followed him to these condos over by the Wharf. I didn't park in the parking lot of the condos. Instead, I parked on the street and made sure to get out of my car first, so he wouldn't notice me. I stood in the shadows and watched him enter the building, then I proceeded to walk to the building. I didn't see what unit he entered. These condos were those garden-styled condos with balconies, so I figured it wouldn't be too hard to figure out which unit he entered. Well, just as I was about to open the door to the building, I heard voices on the balcony just above my head. The male voice was familiar. I stooped down in the dark so that I wouldn't be noticed. Besides, at that time of night, people weren't coming in and out like they would be during the day. I could hear the laughter of a woman, and then I heard her call out for Ramone."

Getting deeply enthralled into this drama, "Oh my word! You had him. Why didn't you bust him then?"

"No. I wanted to see exactly why he was there. Not like I didn't know, but I wanted confirmation. Anyway, slow music was playing and I could see light flickering, like maybe there were candles lit or something. It sounded, from the shuffling of their feet on the concrete, like they were dancing. I could here the smacking of their lips and swapping of spit. Then I hear Ramone tell this woman to bend over the railing. I tried to get as far back in the dark as possible and not say a word. I didn't want her to see me. The woman began to moan and groan and make sighs of passion. I could hear the sounds of smacking, like maybe he was smacking her on her ass or something. My husband was fucking another woman on her balcony for everyone to see, including me." She tried to hold back the tears.

Monica places our meals in front of us. "Anything else I can get for you?"

"No. Nothing else, thank you Monica." Still engulfed in Renee's drama, "Please, continue."

"Well, it was very hard to contain myself. I wanted to run up those stairs, kick open that damn door and beat his ass and hers too. But, I didn't. My mind was going a million miles a minute. Right then and there, I knew I was going to end my marriage because of what I had always assumed was being confirmed, right before my eyes. But Ramone was going to have to pay for it, and pay royally. I needed proof of his infidelity."

"You hired an investigator or something?"

"No, I didn't need to do that."

"Well, other than seeing it with your own eyes, how did you get proof, assuming that you have physical proof that is?"

"Well, one good thing came of his affairs."

"Which is what?"

"He used condoms."

"And that's a good thing?"

"Yes. For one, I never caught an STD and after he finished fucking that bitch, he tossed the condom in the bushes. Dumb ass should've flushed it down the toilet like normal people."

"Wait, you have a two-year-old used condom?"

"Yep!"

Thinking like a physician, "If you didn't preserve it, it won't do you any good."

"Arthur, I've got some sense. I have the used condom safely tucked away in a zip lock bag in a safe deposit box."

"Damn, you've thought of everything, huh?"

"Yes. Despite what Ramone may think, I am always one step ahead of him."

"Well, did you ever put a name to the face of the woman he was with?"

"I certainly did. The next day, I typed in her address on my computer and did a search. Her name is Raven Ward," she said, as I begin to choke on my lobster.

"Are you okay?"

Trying not to reveal my uneasiness with my surroundings and knowing that I definitely can't see this woman anymore, "Yes, I'm fine. It went down the wrong pipe. Are you sure that is the right person? Did you ever approach her or anything? She probably doesn't know that Ramone is married."

"Nope, I don't have to approach her. She probably doesn't know that he is married or maybe she does. But, I really don't care. It's not about her, it's about Ramone going back on the vow he made before me, God and two hundred people. It's about his lies and deceit," she said, as my cell phone vibrates inside my suit pocket. I see by the caller ID that it's Morgan.

"Hi honey!"

"Hi, can you hold one moment please?"

Using my hand to cover the mouth piece, "It's the hospital, do you mind if I take this call in the foyer?"

"Sure, go right ahead."

"Thanks. I won't be but a minute." I found my way to the foyer.

"Hey baby, what's up?"

"Nothing, just wanted to see what time you would be finished with your rounds. Stephanie and I are whipped and ready to go home."

"Okay, I have two more patients to see and I will be done. Give me about an hour. I will call you when I am in front of the building. I don't want you and Stephanie standing outside at this time of night."

"Okay honey. We'll be waiting to hear from you."

"Okay, talk to you shortly. Bye."

"Is everything alright?"

"Yes, everything is fine. Just a follow up call for a patient. So, how's your meal?"

"Delicious! This place is wonderful! Thank you so much for inviting me. You know it's on me," she said, while talking with food in her mouth. That's not very lady-like. Morgan never talks while chewing her food.

"Nope, I wouldn't hear of it."

"Arthur, you paid the last time."

"I know, and I will pay this time too."

"Well, at least let me pay half the bill."

"Nope. But, if it will make you feel better, you can leave the tip."

"Deal."

"How is everything? Can I get you anything else?"

"Everything was wonderful. Renee, would you like dessert or another drink?"

"Nope, I am stuffed!"

"Monica, we'll have the check please."

"Sure, I will tally you up and be right back."

"Arthur, I can't thank you enough for a wonderful evening. Thank you for being a great sounding board."

My attention is focused on the unused silverware. "No problem, Renee. I enjoyed it as well."

"What's wrong, Arthur? Do you need a sounding board too?"

"Renee, I don't quite know how to say this."

Renee forced a half smile. "Easy. Just say it."

"Renee, I hope I didn't lead you on. If I did, that was not my intention. I love my wife and I want to stand true to my vows. I have been fighting with this since the first time I met you. A part of me wants you and the other part knows that I shouldn't be sitting here with you now. You are a very beautiful woman and I would be lying if I said I didn't want to make love to you. But, your husband has put you through so much and I don't want to add to that pain."

"I understand, Arthur and I appreciate you being a man and doing what is right. Your wife is a very lucky woman and I hope she knows that."

"Yes, I think she does."

"This will be our last meal together, huh?"

"Yes, I'm afraid so."

"Well, I must admit that I feel very lucky to have had you in my life, if only for a brief moment. Thank you for everything, and if you ever change your mind, you have my number."

Grabbing her purse and rising up from her seat, Renee walks towards me and gives me a soft kiss on the lips.

"You take care of yourself, Arthur."

Watching Renee walk away, I realize even more that Morgan is truly the love of my life and that Renee didn't leave a tip.

Motioning for Monica, I swallow the rest of my drink, pay the bill and place a twenty-dollar tip in Monica's hand. "Thank you for everything."

Waiting for the valet to arrive with my car, I turn to the voice of my sister-in-law yelling out my name. "Arthur!"

"Well hello stranger, long time no see!" I gave Raven a tight embrace and wondered if this man she is with is Renee's husband.

"Yes, it has been. I thought Morgan told me that you had rounds tonight."

"Ah yeah, I did. I finished them early and stopped down here to have a drink with a colleague, before I head back to the office to pick up Morgan and Stephanie." I look at Raven and then at her friend, wondering if she was going to introduce us.

"Oh, Arthur, this is my friend, Chas. Chas, this is my brother-in-law, Dr. Arthur Carrington."

"Nice to meet you, Chas!" I take a deep sigh of relief and reach for his hand to shake.

"It's a pleasure, Dr. Carrington."

"Please, call me Arthur."

"Okay, Arthur."

"Well, here is my ride. You guys going to have dinner?"

"Yes, I hear this place is great!" Raven said with excitement.

"Yes, it is. Well, Chas, it was nice meeting you. Raven, talk to you later. Enjoy your dinner." I hop in my car and think that this shit is too close for comfort.

16 / the truth hurts

Marcy was not fully over Jay, because she informed me that Jay was trying to rekindle their relationship. Cassie called things off with Marcy, because Marcy's dumb ass was considering taking him back. Cassie felt that if she couldn't have all of Marcy, she didn't want any of her. I can't say that I blame her. After all, I kind of thought I had all of Ramone, seeing as though I could have him whenever I wanted him, but I was wrong. Men are such dogs. Men are the reason why women do such vindictive shit. They make us vindictive.

I must admit, I do feel sorry for Marcy. However, it is nice to see that these doggish ass black men treat white women the same way as they treat black women. Now I don't feel too slighted. I am more convinced, thanks to Marcy, than I was before that the difference between white women and black women is that, after a black woman catches a dog fucking a bitch, she sure as hell won't take his ass back; a white woman would go for that shit. Well, I ain't saying that is a fact, however, Marcy is doing a damn good job of confirming it, that's for damn sure. I tried to be a good influence on her, hoping I could make her see that the dog shit you find on the bottom of your shoe is on a much higher level than Jay Dawson. But, oh well, I guess ol' girl is hooked on the black dick.

Today is going to be a good day. Marcy and I are going to a matinee. I don't care what movie we see, as long as everything goes according to plan. And knowing Marcy and how much of a dunce she really is, my plan will go off without a hitch. I really shouldn't be dragging her into the middle of my beef with Jay, but that motherfucker has got to pay for the shit he did to me in that damn elevator and I won't rest until he does. Yes, today is going to be a good day.

It's been a few days since I've spoken with Morgan. I need to call her and see what she is up to. I've been so deep into Chas, I can't see straight. That man has just been absolutely wonderful. As a matter of fact, I haven't seen nor heard from Ramone since Chas and I have been hanging pretty heavy. I wonder if he knows about us. Well, it ain't like I care if he knows or not. Anyway, what the hell can he say? Not a damn thing, the married bastard!

The fact that Ramone is married doesn't bother me. What hurts me is that he didn't tell me. I mean, he knows all of my business. He knows every aspect of my life. He knows all about my family. Damn, he's been in and out of my bed for going on three years. Didn't I deserve to at least know the truth? Besides, it probably wouldn't have mattered to me if he was married or not, as long as I could have him when I wanted. There isn't a man alive, yet, that has rocked my world like Ramone has. That man has more tricks up his sleeve than a street corner magician.

I wonder if Arthur rocks Morgan. She has never said if he did or didn't, but on the other hand, she ain't never complained either. I am sure he is dickin' her good, with his fine ass. He looks like that pretty motherfucker from that movie *The Best Man*. You know, the one with those pretty eyes. That man makes me moist, and he looks just like Arthur. Hell, a motherfucker that fine got to know how to fuck. Besides, he walks like he has a big dick.

Before I hop in the shower, I decide to call Morgan. Grabbing the cordless phone from its cradle, I press the speed dial button that has Morgan's name labeled beside it. Morgan answered after the sixth ring. "Hey girl, what took you so long to answer the phone? Kind of late for you and Arthur to be getting your Saturday morning groove on, isn't it?" I chuckled.

"Girl, Arthur had to skip his Saturday morning roll in the hay, which was fine with me, because he had a five-thirty tee time with John Howard."

"You mean that fine ass Dr. Howard, who came to your New Year's Eve party last year?"

"Yep. He and Arthur are always playing golf. Arthur says that John is very competitive and his competitiveness makes him not want to play. But, he's a colleague and a good friend, so he grits his teeth and bears it."

"How are you feeling?"

"I am fine. I have a little morning sickness. I'm just glad that Arthur left early enough so that I wouldn't have to puke while he was still home."

"Morgan, you haven't told him yet?"

"No."

"What are you waiting for?"

"Ray, I am afraid to tell him."

"Afraid of what?"

"Afraid of his reaction. He may want me to have an abortion."

"Mo, I don't think he would react like that. You need to tell him so that he can keep his eye on you. He is a doctor, isn't he?"

"Yes, but he is a Urologist, not a Gynecologist."

"Well, hell, they all have to train the same way."

"Whatever, Dr. Ward," she said, as we both laughed.

"Seriously, Mo, exactly how does your doctor feel about this?"

"What do you mean?"

"I know you said that he feels that you will carry this baby full term, but what about after delivery?"

"Well, during the pregnancy, he will be monitoring all of my internal organs. You know, my kidneys, liver, and stuff like that. As long as the baby doesn't put too much of a strain on my internal organs, I should be fine. He is pumping me with every prenatal vitamin on the market, and I go to his office once a week for him to take blood and other stuff. So Ray, don't worry, everything will be fine. Besides, if anything does happen to me, my baby will have a wonderful mother in you."

"Now you are talking stupid Morgan, and I don't want to hear you talk like that ever again! You hear me?" I yelled into the phone.

"Yes ma'am, I hear you and you really need to calm down because all that damn yelling in my ear don't mean shit to me. Do you hear me?" she mimicked, sucking her teeth.

"Mo, I 'm just worried about you. You need to tell Arthur, but I'm sure you will tell him when you feel he needs to know."

"Well, thank you for letting me handle my business."

"You just love kissing my ass, don't you?"

"How can anybody kiss your ass when it never stays in one position?" She cracked herself up with that one.

"Girl, you ain't never lied!"

"So, what's on your agenda for today?"

"Hanging out with Marcy today. We are going to catch a movie and then do dinner." I make sure I don't tell her of my plans. Morgan would deliver that baby right now if she knew that I was about to use Marcy to get back at Jay.

"You aren't seeing Chas tonight? Speaking of Chas, where is Ramone? Is he still in the picture? Girl, I just can't keep up with all of your men folks, Whorina," she said, laughing at my expense.

"One, I am not going to see Chas tonight. I just told you I was hanging out with Marcy. Two, Ramone can go straight to hell. Three, I am only seeing Chas right now. I am ready to settle down for a minute and he just feels right."

"It's about time. And who the hell is Marcy?"

"Marcy is this chick who works with me. She's having female problems, so I am letting her hang with me to get things off her mind."

"Female problems? You mean cramps and shit like that?"

"No Morgan, damn. She is a lesbo and her butch kicked her to the curb."

"Ouch! That's pretty messed up. Is she a sista?"

"Nope."

"Wait, let me get this straight. You, Miss Strictly Dickly, will be hanging out with a lesbian on a Saturday, and a white one at that. You have something up your sleeve, Raven Ward. What is it?"

"I don't have anything up my sleeve. I am just being a friend to her, that's all."

"Ray, your ass doesn't know how to be a friend to nobody, but your damn self."

"Damn Morgan, what are you saying?"

"I am saying that you are the most selfish person I know, and that the only reason why you would befriend this woman is because she has something you need. Now, tell me that my ass is wrong."

"Now see, only you can come out your face and say some fucked up shit like that about me, Morgan. And yes, your ass is wrong."

"No, I don't think that I am, Raven. Just remember, what goes around comes around. If you aren't careful, when it comes back around, it's going to knock you straight on your fucking ass!"

"Damn Sis, I didn't know you felt that way about me. I guess there is nothing left for me to say."

"Raven, you are my sister and I love you with all of my heart, and there is nothing that I wouldn't do for you and you know this. But, as your sister and best friend, and probably your only friend, I can tell you about yourself and continue to love you and accept you for the way that you are. My intentions are not to hurt your feelings. I just want you to see that being vindictive is not always the way to go. Things will work themselves out. If someone does you wrong, you need to pray on it and let it go. He will take care of it. He will work it out. Believe what I say, baby girl. So, whatever it is that you've got planned, please, think twice about it, is all that I am asking."

"I hear you Morgan, and there is nothing going on."

"Okay, if you say so. Raven, just remember what I said."

"Okay Morgan, I hear ya. I gotta run. I need to get ready to meet Marcy. Oh, what are your plans today?"

"I've got some house cleaning to do."

"You need a damn maid. Bye!" I hung up the phone before she could respond.

I heard Morgan loud and clear and she is right. That girl does know me better than I know myself. I couldn't say a word in my defense because she saw right through me and it hurt. But, I can't let this go. Jay will pay for what he did. And, well, as far as Marcy is concerned, it's unfortunate, but anything goes.

17 / payback's a bitch

Arriving at Marcy's place an hour early, knowing that she wouldn't be ready, gives me time to set my plan into action. "Hey Raven, you're early, come on in. As you can see, I'm not quite ready. Make yourself at home and give me ten minutes."

"Sure, Marcy. Sorry I'm early, but I had to run a few errands before coming this way, and I thought it would take me longer than it did. I hope you don't mind."

"No, not at all. Help yourself to the kitchen. I'll be out in a few."

"Thanks girl." I look around for the telephone.

After two years, Jay's phone number had not changed. Dialing his number from memory, I can't help but play back Morgan's words in my mind. Morgan doesn't understand and she never will. I've got to do this.

While listening out for Marcy, Jay's voice plays in my ear from his answering service. *"Hi, this is Jay. At the beep, leave a message."*

"Hi Jay, this is Marcy. I've been thinking about you and I want to see you. If you don't have any plans tonight, I would love for you to come over around eight o'clock. When you get this message, call me and leave a message. I will be out most of the day. Bye." I recited that like a professional.

Returning to the sofa in the living room and looking around the small one-bedroom apartment that is decorated with warm earth tones and '70s décor. For a white chick, this girl sure has a lot of ethnic knick-knacks. An oak-framed picture of Marcy and a black woman stands on one of the four glass shelves that are encased by tarnished brass that could stand a good cleaning. Thinking that the woman in the picture is probably Cassie, I walk over to get a closer look. Damn, that must be Cassie 'cause she looks like a damn dike.

Marcy was excited about having a girls day out. "Okay, I'm ready!"

"Great, let's rock and roll."

After the movies, Marcy and I decide to have lunch and do some shopping. That girl has absolutely no taste, whatsoever. She needs to get the hell out of the '70s and bring her ass up to the year 2000. Just because trends repeat itself, doesn't mean you have to follow suit. After spending the whole day with Marcy, I find that she is so hooked on Jay, he could fuck her mother and it wouldn't make a difference to her, so long as she had him back in her life. I still can't believe she is going to take him back. This chick is mixed up.

We arrive back at her place at six o'clock with a bag of movies that we rented from the Video Den and junk food to pig out on.

"Whew, I've got to use your bathroom. I've been holding this for three hours."

"You aren't by yourself. You're company you can go first. I can wait."

Noticing that the red light on her answering machine was flashing, I insist that she goes first. Once I heard the bathroom door close, I leapt towards the answering machine. Turning down the volume, placing my ear to the speaker, I hold my breath and press the play button.

"Yo Marcy, this is Jay. I got your message. I knew you would change your mind and come to your senses. Pussy ain't enough to sustain you, huh? Listen baby, I will be there at eight o'clock sharp. I want you ready and waiting, butt-naked, spread eagle on your bed. I will use my key. It's been a while and I know that you need a good fucking from a man."

That motherfucker. I erase the tape and walk towards the kitchen to put the junk food away. Damn, he talked like Marcy was a piece of meat; like she couldn't make it without his ass. Who does he think he is? I hear the toilet flush and within seconds, Marcy is in the kitchen. "Okey dokey, it's all yours." She is such a perky ass.

"Thanks girl." While using the bathroom, I think that Jay deserves what I am about to throw on his ass. Heading back towards the living room, I notice that Marcy was already pigging out on the bag of potato chips.

"Girl, save me some."

"Ray, grab the sodas and some ice, please."

I look at my watch and notice the time ticking away fast. "Sure." One thing about Jay, he is always on time, so I need to rush this along. "How about a drink instead?"

"I don't have anything in the house to drink, Raven."

"Sure you do. I picked up something while we were out, remember?"

"Oh yeah. Well, make mine a double!"

"You ain't said nothing but a word. Coming up!"

Marcy's kitchen is spotless and everything is organized down to the alphabetized spice rack. Damn, this bitch has issues. As I close the freezer door, the theme to the *Twilight Zone* plays in my head. I hand Marcy her drink. "Here we go. You have any matches?"

"Yeah, I think so. Check over there on the coffee table."

"Girl, let me find out you have some 'oldies but goodies' hiding over here!" I light my joint and flip through Marcy's record collection.

"Yeah, since you're over there, put something on." She took her fourth sip. If I didn't know any better, I would think Marcy was getting in the mood for something. After putting on some music, I take my seat beside her and glance at my watch. "So Raven, tell me something about yourself." Marcy asked as she reaches for the joint.

Damn, she is getting into this. Is this working in my favor or what? "Well, what do you want to know?"

"Whatever you want to tell me."

"Well, ask me something and I will give you an answer, how about that?"

"Okay. What's your favorite color?"

"Pastels are my favorite."

"What's your sign?"

"Virgo."

"You have any sisters or brothers?"

I take a toke from the joint and watch Marcy refill her glass for the second time. "One sister."

"Do you like women?"

Bingo! I was waiting for that. Looking at my watch, I see that an hour has passed. It won't be long now. "Yes, I like women."

"Really? I thought you were strictly into men."

"I am."

"Well, how can you like women?"

"I like women as friends and friends only."

"Oh, I see. Well, have you ever thought about being with a woman?"

"Yes." I lied through my teeth. The thought of being with a woman is really starting to sicken me. But, a girl gotta do what a girl gotta do.

"And what have you thought?"

"Well, I've always wondered if it would be the same as being with a man."

"No it's not the same." She stroked my cheek. "Being with a man is rough and intensely physical, with a lot of pounding. But with a woman, the act of making love is just that, making love. Its sensuous and there is no pounding, only stroking, caressing, sucking and licking." She slid closer to me.

I bring myself to gaze into her eyes. "Are you trying to show me, Marcy?" She is making the first move, so now I don't feel so bad about using her. Besides, after hearing Jay's message, I'm doing this for her as much as I'm doing it for me.

"Yes." She leans in towards me and caresses my lips with hers. I think that I may throw up any minute.

Quickly pulling back and having second thoughts about this freaky shit, "Marcy, this is all very new to me. I've never kissed a woman in an intimate way before."

"Ray, relax. Close your eyes and think of me as being a man. It's very sensual. Trust me."

Taking a deep breath and closing my eyes, Marcy strokes the side of my face. Closing my eyes, I suck on her finger. Moving herself closer to me, she grabs the back of my head and pulls my face into hers. Pressing her lips against mine, her tongue breaks through and begins to play around inside my mouth. Relaxing myself and succumbing to her touches, she unbuttons my top with one hand while the other hand is roaming up and down my thighs. Still kissing me, she cups my breast in her hand and begins to squeeze my nipple between her fingers.

"How does it feel, Raven?"

Without a sound, I move closer, taking her into me. The heaving of my body answers her question. She stands up and motions for me to follow her to the bedroom. "No, I want to stay right here." I'm lying flat on the floor, motioning for her to come and lay beside me.

"In a minute. I have something for you and I know you will like it."

Marcy heads to her bedroom and returns with a big, black dildo in her hand. Kneeling before me, she bends down and kisses me with full passion, while slipping her hands inside my panties and stroking my clit with her middle finger. With my eyes closed, I begin to move my hips against her fingers. Wanting to hurry this along, I take off my pants and instruct Marcy to do the same. To my surprise, Marcy straps on the dildo.

"Are you going to fuck me with that, Marcy?"

"Yes." The palms of her hands rest on my knees. " Spread your legs."

"I will on one condition."

"And that is?"

"You suck my clit first. I love to have my clit sucked."

"Well, you are a guest in my house."

Lying face down on the floor, with her face in my pussy, she spreads my lips apart with her fingers, taking my clit in her mouth, gently sucking it. I grab the back of her head and grind my hips into her face, "Yes baby, damn this feels good. Damn, you are going to make me cum!"

Marcy stops sucking my clit and climbs on top of me, "I want to cum with you."

I've never used a dildo before. "How are you going to do that?"

Marcy reaches down between my legs and inserts the dildo into my sopping wet pussy. "The dildo has a clit stimulator."

She is actually fucking me and I am enjoying it. Does this mean that I am turning into a lesbo? Tasting my flavor on her tongue, Marcy strokes me with intense passion. Wrapping my legs around her waist, I pull her into my hips and join her rhythm.

"Does it feel good baby?"

"Yes, it feels wonderful." I could barely catch my breath.

"I want you on top of me."

"You want me to fuck you?" I asked, looking into her eyes.

"Yes, I do. As you can see, there is nothing to it."

"But…"

"Hush." She kissed me. "I want you to make me cum, Ray."

"I don't eat pussy Marcy, sorry."

"You don't have to. I want to come with you inside me. Here, strap this around your waist." She removes the dildo and hands it to me.

"Well, you could've waited until I came before you pulled out."

"Trust me. You will cum."

Looking at the clock on the wall and realizing that I have exactly five minutes before Jay walks through the door, I grab the dildo and strap it around my waist. With Marcy's guidance, I found myself on top of her, stroking her and enjoying every minute of it. The intensity builds as my clit is being stimulated with every thrust I make. Damn, this shit is getting too good to me now. Looking into Marcy's eyes, something comes over me. "I want your ass in the air. Assume the bitch position." I yank her up off of the floor.

"Ooh Ray, I see you are getting into this. I like this side of you."

Seeing her lily white ass in my face, visions of my ancestors being raped and beaten, takes control of my common sense. It's time for a little payback. Pulling her ass towards me, I insert the dildo inside her, stroking with full force. Damn, no wonder men like the doggie position, this shit is arousing the hell out of me. "Do you like the way I'm fucking you?" I smack her on the ass.

"Oh yes!"

"Marcy! Do you like this big, black dick in you?" I yell with vengeance in my voice.

"Yes!" She turned to look at me.

"Bitch, turn the fuck around. Don't look at me!" I pinch her ass as hard as I can. Grabbing her hair, I pull her head back and continue thrusting this piece of rubber that I have taken on as an extension of me. Shoving my finger in her mouth, I take her saliva and rub it around her asshole, making it moist. Closing my eyes, I insert my finger. "Loosen that asshole up, girl." Removing my finger from her asshole, wiping her waste on her sofa, I insert the dildo.

"Raven!"

Not hearing her, in my own world, enraged, I continue to build my momentum, giving her an open-handed smack to her right butt cheek with every thrust. The ear piercing cries coming from Marcy breaks my concentration. I stop. "Marcy, am I hurting you?"

"No, I love it! Don't stop you black bitch! Fuck me!"

She didn't say black bitch, did she? With that echoing through my mind, I commenced to fuck that bitch just the way she wants. My thrusts are hard and forceful. With each thrust, I am getting closer and closer to my climax. We both are moaning and groaning with pleasure.

"I'm about to cum, Marcy!"

"I want to cum with you, Raven."

"Rub your clit, bitch!"

With a few powerful thrusts and Marcy rubbing her clit, our moans grow louder drowning out the music, and our movements are more forceful. "Oh shit!" Marcy yelled. "Fuck me, Raven. Fuck me, bitch!" With one last power thrust to her asshole, my body begins to shake, as I cum inside the dildo. My body goes limp from exhaustion and rests on Marcy's back.

"What the fuck is this?" came from the front door.

"I just finished fucking your girl," I said, as Marcy shuffles to her feet.

"Marcy, what the fuck is going on?" Jay asked with anger in his eyes.

While Marcy attempts to explain to Jay why I had a dildo in her ass, I gather my clothes, walk towards Marcy, grab her by the waist, stick my tongue down her throat, smack her on the ass and tell her to handle her business. Turning to walk out the door, I stop for Jay to step to the side. Staring into his eyes, I move closer towards him. Pulling myself up on my toes, I whisper into his ear. "Don't you dare put your fucking hands on her. That's my bitch now. My pussy is all over her face."

With so much scorn and hatred in his eyes, "You heartless bitch!" he snarled between clenched teeth. "You will pay for this."

"Anything goes, right Jay?" I blow him a kiss and walked out of Marcy's apartment.

18 / a fucked-up ego

Turning to face me, with pure hatred in his eyes, "Is that the kind of shit you like, Marcy?" Jay yelled as he slammed the door in my face.

"Jay, let me explain!" Marcy sounds as though she is shuffling around trying to get away from him.

"What the fuck is there to explain? How the fuck can you explain the fact that I walk into my bitches place and find another bitch fucking her in the ass with a fucking dildo? Yeah, explain that shit to me, Marcy!" Jay knocks over the lamp that used to sit on the end table beside the sofa.

"First of all Jay, I am not your bitch! We are over, remember? Oh, wait! The table has turned, huh? Wasn't I the one who walked through that same door and found you fucking Cassie in my bed? As I recall, she was ass up too!" She threw a glass that shattered from the impact of it hitting the door.

"You are just like the rest of the bitches; you are no different."

With my ear plastered to her front door, I try to slip on my clothes. "Jay, I will not have you disrespect me in my own home! I am not your bitch and I will never be your bitch. This bitch is too good for your black ass!" I heard Marcy exclaim. No she didn't. The last thing a black man wants to hear is a white person, any white person, calling him a black anything. Those are fighting words.

"What the fuck did you just say to me you nasty white whore?" Jay had scorn in his voice. "Bitch, do you know I will fuck you up?"

"Jay, I think you'd better leave." Her voice was calm.

Tossing a chair to the side, he yelled, "Oh, fuck that shit. You like to be ass up, huh, with rubber up your ass? And, black rubber at that?"

"Jay, no! Please, no!"

"Come here!"

"Please Jay, don't do this! I promise, it won't happen again."

"You damn right it won't happen again, because I am going to see to that shit right now. Now, I said, come here!"

"Okay Jay, just calm down. I'll do whatever you want, just calm down, okay baby." She slipped into her jeans.

"Oh, now I'm your baby. Well, okay baby...oh fuck that, don't put your clothes on now."

"Jay, I'm cold. I need to put my clothes on."

"Oh, now you're cold? You weren't cold when that bitch was heating up your asshole, now were you? You need to be warmed up again?" Jay unzipped his pants and dropped them to his knees. "Suck my dick, bitch!"

"Jay, I…"

"Shut the fuck up! The only thing I want to hear is you sucking on this big, black dick, you understand me? Now, get on your knees and crawl over here and do as I say."

"Jay, listen baby…"

"Marcy, I am already angry with you. Please, don't make it worse. Do as I say. I would hate to have to whip your ass because you can't follow simple directions. Now, for the last time…" Marcy knelt down before Jay's dick and took him in her mouth. Jay grabbed the back of Marcy's head and began fucking her mouth with full force. Jay gave Marcy an open-handed slap to the face. "Ouch! Bitch! You trying to bite my dick off?" Grabbing her hair, he stares into her eyes with the look of death. "Bitch, you will pay for that shit!" He took his fist to her ear, drawing blood. Marcy howls. "Turn your ass around, I'ma let you see what a real dick feels like."

Wanting to get it over with, Marcy does what she is told. Already kneeling on the floor, Marcy places the flat of her palms to the floor. "Jay, you will need lubricant," she said through numbness and tears. He looks at her with disgust and walks towards the kitchen and retrieves a bottle of cooking oil. Returning to see Marcy's badly irritated anus pointing directly at him, for a minute, he feels sorry for her until her words "black ass" runs rampant through his mind. He pours half the bottle of cooking oil between the crack of her ass. She begins to cry. "Why are you doing this to me, Jay?"

Her question stinging his mind, he walks towards her face and kneels down before her. Lifting her up from her knees, he gives a black stare into her eyes. "I treat whores like whores." Turning on his heels, he walks toward the door, but suddenly stops in his tracks. Looking over his shoulder and seeing her in her nakedness and embarrassment, "I feel sorry for you because you had no idea the lengths that Raven would go to get revenge on me."

"Revenge? Why would Raven want to get revenge on you? She doesn't even know you!"

"She knows me and I know her."

Marcy stands to her feet. "I don't understand."

"I used to fuck that bitch long before you were in the picture and she got beside herself and wanted to fuck me in the damn elevator. I guess she called herself having control over me, but that bitch was wrong, dead wrong. She is the one who ended up getting fucked and I fucked her real good too. So now, she got her revenge because it fucked me up to see that bitch fucking you in your asshole. You are trash and she is the trash collector. Clean yourself up. You look a fucking mess." Opening the front door, Jay is startled by my presence. Gazing into my eyes, he builds saliva in his throat. Forming a wad in his mouth, he spits in my face. "You cunt," he snarled, taking off down the hall and out the door of Marcy's apartment building.

"Are you okay?" I asked Marcy.

Looking past me, without an utter, Marcy closes the door in my face.

19 / *its too late*

L eaving Marcy's place, I ride home in silence. I should be relishing in the joy of seeing the look on Jay's face when he saw me with a dildo in Marcy's ass. But instead, I really feel like shit. Damn, the guilt of putting Marcy in the middle of this is eating me up. Marcy was an innocent bystander and I took advantage of her weakness. I pick up my car phone to call Morgan, but I dial Marcy's number instead. Maybe I will feel better if I could just say that I'm sorry.

"Yes," Marcy answered the phone with numbness.

"Marcy?"

"What do you want?"

"Marcy, I want to make sure you're alright."

"I'm fine."

"I don't believe you. Can I please come back to see for myself?"

"Why, haven't you done enough already?"

"Marcy please. I feel awful."

"Good."

"Marcy, please, I need to see you. Please."

"Go to hell, Raven."

"Okay, I deserved that. I was wrong. Please, give me the opportunity to right a wrong."

"Hahahahahahahahaha! Now, that is some real funny shit."

"Marcy, please," I begged, trying not to sound irritated.

"Fine."

"Great, I will be there in a few minutes."

Placing my car phone back in its cradle, I search my mind for a way to smooth things over with Marcy. Turning on my radio to calm me, the melodic voice of D.C.'s top on-air personality, Lee Jackson, calls off slow jams on his play list. Thinking of nothing but Marcy and how I am going to smooth things over with her, my cell phone rings, "Hello."

"Hey baby, where are you?"

"Hi Chas! I'm on my way to Marcy's place."

"Oh? You should be leaving there by now, right? Weren't you two together all day?"

"Yeah baby, we were and I was on my way home, but I realized I left my purse, so I'm going back to pick it up."

"Okay, cool. Listen, if you aren't too tired, why don't you come on over after you leave Marcy's. I could use some of your sweet company."

"Sounds like a plan to me."

"Good, I will see you soon."

"Yes. Oh, and Chas?"

"Yes baby."

"I'm going to stop by my place and pick up a little overnight bag, okay?"

"Sounds like music to my ears baby."

"Okay, and baby?"

"Yes," he says with a chuckle.

"I'm really, really into you."

"That's good to hear, Ray. We will talk when you get here. Just hurry up and get here. I miss you something awful. Kiss, kiss."

Thinking Chas is the perfect end to a horrible night, I quickly pull into Marcy's complex wanting to get in, get out and get dicked. Standing at Marcy's front door, I take in a deep breath and exhale. Lights, camera, action.

"Come in and make it quick," she said, opening the door before I could knock.

"Oh my God. Marcy, what did he do to you?"

"Nothing that you didn't do."

"What?"

"You heard me."

"But what happened between us, I thought you wanted to happen."

"Well, anything goes, right Raven. Those are the words you said to Jay, right?"

"Marcy, no, you misunderstood what I said to him."

"Oh? Well why don't you fucking clarify what I misunderstood."

"Marcy, I told Jay that you belonged to me and that he better not put his fucking hands on you or he would regret it," I said, holding my breath and hoping that she would believe that bullshit.

"You did?" She is so damn gullible.

Walking towards her and about to lay it on really thick, "Yes, I did. Marcy, what we shared tonight was special. You introduced me to a new, exciting world. You introduced me to the Marcy that I want to continue to see." I am not believing the words coming out of my mouth.

"You do?"

Attempting to turn the tables, I keep my fingers crossed and hope that this shit works. "Yes, I do. Look Marcy, I didn't know Jay was going to come over. One minute I am into loving you and making you feel good and the next, he is standing in the doorway. Baby, why does he still have a key to your place?"

"I don't know. I guess I never thought about getting it back." She looks dumbfounded.

I wipe the tears from her eyes. "Baby, I think you should get your key from Jay or better yet, I don't want you coming into contact with him again. Why don't you call building management and tell them you need to have your locks changed. Okay, baby? I would hate for him to walk in on us again. Okay?

"Okay Ray. I'll do that first thing in the morning."

"That's good baby. That's real good." I smile and give her a kiss on the lips to seal the deal.

"Ray, will you stay with me tonight? I don't want to be alone."

"Baby, I can't. As I was coming back to see you, I got a call from my sister and she's not doing so well. She's pregnant and her husband is doing night rounds at the hospital. She's not handling this pregnancy too well and she asked me to come and stay with her tonight. I'm sorry, honey. Let's make plans for another night." I kiss her on the cheek and lips.

"Okay, if that is how it must be."

I turn on my heels to make a fast exit. "I'm afraid so, sweetie."

"Raven?"

"Yes Marcy."

"Why did you use me?"

"What? I did not use you, Marcy."

"Why didn't you tell me that you used to fuck Jay?"

"Is that what he told you? Look, baby, I don't..."

"No! Keep your lies to yourself, Raven. Do you take me for a dumb white girl? Do you think that I am that stupid?"

I am desperately searching for the right words. "Marcy, you've got this all wrong!"

"Oh? No, I don't think so, Raven. But you know what? It's all good because I'm fine. I don't need Jay and I sure as hell don't need you!" She threw a lamp at my head.

"What the fuck?" I ducked. "Bitch, I think you have lost your fucking mind and you need to chill the fuck out."

"No! You need to come clean with me, Raven!"

"Marcy, I don't know what you are talking about!"

"Jay told me about the elevator! He told me that you made a move on him and he didn't want your advances, but you insisted he fuck you right there in the fucking elevator and he did! He fucked you without regard for your feelings and you didn't like it! Isn't that right, Raven? Just like you did me tonight, huh?" I stood there speechless.

"Answer me, you cunt!"

"Okay, okay! Yes, all of it is true! I had to make him pay for what he did to me in that elevator!"

"No, you had to make him pay for what you did to yourself!"

"I didn't fuck myself in that elevator, Marcy! I didn't make myself bend over with my palms flat on the floor and keep my knees in a locked position while I fucked myself! He raped me in the elevator!"

"Raven, do you ever take responsibility for your own actions? What happened in that elevator was that you lost control of the situation. The tables turned and instead of Jay getting fucked, you did. But, I wasn't in the elevator. I didn't have anything to do with what you did to yourself. You were wrong for taking it out on me. You befriended me, you pretended to care about me and about my feelings. You don't care about anyone, but Raven!" She walked towards the bathroom. Her words stung.

"Marcy, where are you going? Listen to me, it is not what you think. I do care about you and your feelings, despite what happened here tonight. I was wrong, I was dead wrong for putting you in the middle, but I did it for you too! Don't you see that?"

Marcy turns towards me and gives me the look of death. "You did it for me?" she growled. "You ain't do shit for me!"

"Yes, I did." An uneasiness came over me.

"How dare you! How dare you say that! You don't do shit for anyone else, but yourself!"

"Not true Marcy, really. Jay did nothing but humiliate you and treat you as though you were less than he was. For God sakes, you caught him with another woman in your bed! Marcy, Jay left a message for you, saying that he was coming over here at eight o'clock and he wanted you butt-naked, on your bed, spread eagle. Now, if that is not humiliation and treating you like trash, I don't know what is!" I watch Marcy's body go limp as tears begin to stream down her face.

"What message?"

"Marcy, I…"

"Jay was right. You set him up and me too."

"Marcy no, that's not true."

"Oh save it, Ray. This has nothing to do with Jay. It has to do with you and me. Don't you get it?"

"Marcy, please…"

"No, I suppose you don't. Raven, I don't allow anyone to fuck me in my ass unless I have feelings for them. I gave myself to you. I expressed my innermost feelings to you by tasting you and exploring you and you exploring me. Raven, I love you."

"You love me?" I think I need a Q-tip, I may have ear wax buildup. What is with everyone and this love thing?

"I did, until you pulled this shit."

"Marcy, I don't know what to say."

"I didn't expect that you would. It seems as if every time I develop feelings for someone, they step all over them; wiping their feet all over me. I am not dog shit on the bottom of your shoe, Raven. I have feelings and I loved you!" She runs down the hall and closes the bathroom door behind her.

"Marcy?"

"Marcy, please open the door. Let's talk this out. I didn't know you felt that way about me. I've never had anyone, other than my sister, to love me."

"Fuck you, Raven! It's too late. I don't want your ass now. I was all wrong about you. I thought you were different, but you're not. You are no different than Jay or Cassie! Leave me alone!"

"Marcy, please open the door!" I was yelling against dead silence. "Marcy! Marcy!" Getting nervous from not hearing any sounds from the other side of the door, I attempt to knock the door open with my shoulder, "Ouch! Marcy, open the fucking door!"

"Go away, Raven. It's too late." Her voice was low and drawn out. Looking around for something to open the door with, I go into the living room and pick up the chair that is placed in front of the dining room table. Making my way back down the hallway towards the bathroom door, I raise the chair in front of me and with full force, I ram the chair into the door. Marcy was right, it was too late. Marcy lay in her bathtub, in a pool of fresh blood that came from the self-inflicted slashes in her wrists, ankles and throat.

20 / the clean up woman

I have got to get a grip. I don't believe this shit. Why would Marcy go and do some dumb shit like this? She doesn't have a pulse and I don't know CPR. What in the hell do I do? Okay, this is not the time for me to panic. I have got to gather my bearings and think. After covering Marcy's body with the shower curtain, I run to the kitchen to use Marcy's phone. On second thought, I better use my cell phone. "Morgan."

"What's wrong, Ray?"

"Oh, thank God you're home. I have really fucked up, Mo. I don't know what to do."

"First of all, calm down and tell me exactly what is going on."

"Morgan, she's dead."

"Who's dead, Ray! Who are you talking about?"

"Marcy, she's dead. Mo, Marcy killed herself."

"What do you mean she killed herself?"

"She killed herself! Marcy slashed herself up!"

"How, why…Ray, where are you?"

"I'm at Marcy's place."

"Ray, tell me what happened?"

"No."

"Why not?"

"Because…"

"Because what, Raven?"

"Because I don't want you to say 'I told you so'."

"No I won't."

"Yes you will," I said, crying into the phone.

"Okay Ray, you are making me very nervous. Now please, tell me what happened to Marcy. Take a few deep breaths and tell me the whole story."

"No, I can't, not right now. I've got to get out of here!"

"Are you there alone?"

"Yes."

"Before you leave, make sure you take a rag or something and wipe down every item you've touched and every place you sat your ass. Hell, if she has a fucking vacuum cleaner, use it. Make sure you cover your hands with something before you touch it. You didn't step in any blood, did you?"

"No. No, I don't think so." I am shocked at the orders Morgan is barking at me. I've never seen her like this before.

"Double check to make sure. Where is her body?"

"Morgan, I'm scared. I don't know what to do. I didn't do it."

"Ray, it's going to be okay. Where is her body?"

"In the bathtub."

"Did you touch her at all?"

"Morgan, please help me," I whimpered.

"I am trying to do that, Ray. Answer me, did you touch her?"

"No! I didn't touch her. I was too afraid."

"Okay, you know I have your back." Morgan took a deep breath and exhaled. "Where does Marcy live?"

"Larchmont Square, apartment 206."

"Okay, I am on my way. Remember what I told you, Ray. Clean up! If you touched a glass, wash it in very, very hot water and scrub that bitch as if you are trying to scrub off a layer of fucking glass, you got me?"

"Yes."

"Good! Get yourself together. This is no time for you to sit over there and wallow in your own shit. Don't you open the fucking door unless it's me, got it?"

"Yes, I got it."

"Good."

"Mo?"

"Yeah?"

"Hurry up!"

"I will be there in twenty minutes."

Not knowing which way to turn, I attempt to do as Morgan instructed. With shaky hands, I grab the dishrag from the kitchen and begin to wipe down everything that I had touched or sat on. I proceed to wash all of the dishes, wipe down the kitchen, vacuum the carpet and the furniture, and dust the dining room table. I continue to alphabetize her album collection and wipe down each and every one. Remembering that I used the toilet earlier, I head to the bathroom to clean, trying to keep my mind off of Marcy's naked body immersed in blood, staring at me. Envisioning myself sitting behind bars and being cradled by a woman named Big Bertha, I feel myself on the verge of having a panic attack. After cleaning Marcy's place from top to bottom, I am in need of a drink. "Morgan, where are you? Please, hurry up!" I say aloud as I pace the floor, wringing my hands together and wondering what the fuck was going to happen next. This is what I get for being so fucking vindictive!

This shit is all Jay's fault. If he hadn't done what he did, I wouldn't be standing here right now about to piss my pants! He has got to pay for this shit! Marcy's words played over and over in my head. *"Raven, do you ever take responsibility for your own actions?" "Ray, you don't think about anyone, but yourself."* "Shut up! Shut the fuck up!" I yelled at the voices surrounding me. I can't take this anymore. If Morgan doesn't get here soon, I'm going to lose it. With tears and snot running down my face, I pace the living room floor, looking around and making sure that I haven't forgotten to clean something. The ring from my cell phone startles me. I stare at the phone, wondering if I should answer it. Trying to calm down, I retrieve my cell phone from the coffee table. Checking caller ID, I see that the call is coming from Ramone, so I don't answer. A few minutes later, the phone rings again. This time, it's Chas. I answer the phone as calm as one could, under these conditions.

"Ray, honey where are you?"

"Hi. Um, I am at home, packing a few things, remember?"

"I just called you at home, why didn't you answer your phone?"

"Oh, I must've been in the shower. Yeah, I wanted to freshen up first."

"Oh, okay. Well its getting late Ray, what time do you think you will be here? I don't want you out too late alone. You know how I worry about my baby."

"I know and it won't be much longer. I just need to tie up a few loose ends here at home. I will call you when I'm leaving out," I said, feeling slightly relaxed.

"Okay, don't take too long. I miss you."

"Oh, I miss you too baby," I said with a sigh and pressing the call-end button.

After hearing Chas' voice, I began to cry, wondering what he would think of me. Would he still want me after knowing the type of person I am? Would he even want to speak to me? Do I tell him? How can I go to him tonight and be intimate after dealing with this shit? "Damn you, Marcy! Why did you do this? Why would you go and end your life and fuck up everybody else's?" I yell through clenched teeth, trying my best to knock a hole in the wall with my fist.

"Ray, open the door. It's me, Morgan," I heard coming from the front door.

I wanted confirmation, because I'm not taking any chances. "Morgan?"

"Yes, baby girl, it's me. Open up."

"Oh Ray! It's going to be alright baby." Morgan embraced me.

I feel safer now than ever before. "Mo, I did everything you told me to do. I cleaned real good."

"Good. That's good baby." Looking me up and down, "Ray, I thought you said you didn't touch the body?"

"I didn't." Feeling myself becoming hysterical, "What's wrong?"

"Nothing. Nothing is wrong. Calm down. You just have a little blood on the front of your shirt."

"Oh shit! No, oh my God!"

"Ray, cut it out and don't bring God into your mess." Morgan said, slapped me across the face. "You have got to get control of yourself. This is not like you to not have control!"

Feeling the warmth of the imprint of her hand on my cheek, "Yes, you're right."

"Okay, first of all, let's do a once over of this place. Let's make sure that you have nothing laying around anywhere. Where were you sitting?"

"Over there," I said, pointing to the floor. "In front of the sofa."

"Okay, looks good," she said, inspecting the area. "What about drinks, did you have drinks? Did you wash the glasses? Did you touch a bottle or anything?"

"Yes, yes and yes."

"Good. Where is the trash bag?"

"Huh?"

"The fucking trash, where is it, Ray?"

"It's in the kitchen in the trash can."

"Get it! Don't leave shit in this place." She walks towards the bathroom.

"Morgan, no don't go in there!"

"Shut up, Ray! I've got to make sure everything is straight!" Standing in the doorway of the bathroom, "Did you clean in here?"

"Yes, I did." I begin trembling like a child who was about to be told to go outside and get a switch.

"Oh stop it, Ray! Stop the crying. You can't think when you're crying. You need a clear head. You understand me?"

"Yes. I'm just scared and I want to get out of here."

"I know you are and we can't leave until we are finished taking care of business. Why is the shower curtain covering her?"

"Well, I covered her body because I didn't want to see her exposed like that."

"Fuck! Ray, I told you not to touch the fucking body, damn!"

"I know and I'm sorry, but..."

"Okay, forget it. Take this towel, wet it with hot, soapy water and wipe down the shower curtain."

" Why?"

"To get rid of your fucking prints, that's why!" She looked at me with disgust. "After you do that, take that towel and put it in the trash bag sitting by the door. Where is the rag you used to wipe down everything else?"

"It's in the kitchen. I used the dish rag."

"Get it and put that in the trash too." She stared into my eyes as if she was trying to find a bug that flew in and got lost in the mucus. "Ray, did you smoke that shit tonight?"

"What shit?"

"Ray, look, right now is not the time to act dumb. You know what the fuck I'm talking about. Did you smoke weed tonight?"

"Well, um..."

"Did you or didn't you?"

"Yes, we did."

"Where?"

"Over there, by the sofa, where we sat on the floor."

"Did you vacuum like I told you?"

Walking over towards the sofa, Morgan knelt down on her knees and began inspecting the carpet. "What the fuck is this?" She walks towards me holding the black dildo she found lodged under the sofa.

"I...I don't know."

"You are a lying ass bitch!" She strikes me across the face again. "I am so sick and tired of cleaning up your shit, Raven. Now, rub down the vacuum cleaner, throw those rags in the trash and take off that bloody ass shirt and put on this tee shirt." She pulled out a clean tee shirt from her purse. "Hurry up!"

"I'm moving as fast as I can Morgan," I snapped, because I am getting sick and tired of her ordering me around. Hell, this is not the Army and she is not the Sergeant.

"Oh, hold the fuck up! I know damn well you aren't getting pissy with me, are you?"

"No, I'm not."

"Bitch, you better not. I will only say this once." She walked towards me with her finger pointing in my face. "If I ever hear that you and that corpse in there did some freaky shit before she sliced herself up, I will fuck you up and fuck you up good, you got that?"

"Yes." I nodded my head in disbelief. This was a side of Morgan that I never knew existed.

"Good. Grab that fucking trash bag and let's get the fuck out of here," she said, using the inside of her shirt to open the door.

"But don't we have to call the police or something, and let them know that she is here?"

"Have you lost your fucking mind?" She looks me up and down and rolls her eyes. "Oh yeah, we will call the police and make sure your ass is standing right beside the body with the razor blade in your hand, because I know damn well that girl didn't kill herself just for the hell of it! Now, walk your dumb ass to your car like ain't shit happen and drive the fuck home! Go to Chas, go somewhere, just get the fuck out of my damn face and don't call me! I will call you when I am ready to talk to you!" The door closes behind us, shutting Marcy out of my life for good.

21 / lost and found

Stephanie called over the intercom, as I was reviewing a patient's file. "Dr. C., you have a call on line three."

"Stephanie, I asked not to be disturbed. Please take a message or ask Morgan to take the call."

"Dr. C., Morgan is on the other line and Mr. Walker says that it is pertinent that he speaks with you and you only."

"Mr. Walker? That name doesn't sound familiar, is he a patient?"

"No, he isn't. Will you take the call?" she asked, sounding annoyed with my questions.

"Okay, I'll take the call. Thank you Stephanie." I pressed line three. "Dr. Carrington."

"Hello Arthur, thank you for taking my call. I know you are very busy, but I think we have a problem."

"Problem? First of all, who am I speaking with?"

"Oh, sorry, this is Chas."

"Raven's friend, Chas?"

"Yes."

"Okay, what's the problem?"

"Arthur, have you or Morgan spoken with Raven lately?"

"Well, I haven't spoken with Raven since the night we ran into each other at the Seafood Club. I am sure Morgan has spoken with her, they talk constantly."

"Well, something doesn't sit right with me. Saturday night, Raven didn't show up and it's Wednesday and I haven't heard from her. I've called and called and I'm not getting an answer. Her answering machine doesn't pick up either."

"Well, did you go by her place?"

"Yes, I did…three times. Each time, I knocked until my knuckles turned red and I got no answer. I know she's there because her car is in the parking lot. Arthur please, I'm worried. I called her job and they haven't heard from her either. Something isn't right. It's not like her to be unreachable. She isn't answering her cell phone either."

"Okay man, calm down. Morgan is in the next office. Hold on and I'll ask her about Raven." I place Chas on hold and think that maybe Raven was intentionally avoiding him and I should mind my business. However, it really isn't Raven's M.O. to avoid anyone. If she doesn't want to be bothered, she gives you a good cussing out and that's the end of it. Walking to Morgan's office, I see that the door is ajar. Just as I am about to knock, I overhear her phone conversation. It sounds like my baby is crying.

"Ray, I asked you not to call me. It's not about you, it's about this baby and me. Hell Ray, I haven't even told Arthur that he is going to be a father, because I am too busy trying to keep your black ass out of jail," she said through tears. "Ray, it is time for you to stand up and take responsibility for your own actions. I don't care how you do it, but you need to do it and do it without me. Ray, you come with too much stress and I don't need that right now. I think you need to seek help from someone else, because I am tired. I am just tired. Please, do as I ask and don't call me anymore. I will call you when I am ready to talk. Goodbye Raven." Morgan hangs up the phone and begins to cry in the palms of her hands. "God, please give me strength."

"Baby."

"Um, yes Arthur, what is it?" She searched for tissue to wipe her face.

"Morgan, is everything alright? Were you talking to Ray on the phone?"

"Yes baby, everything is just fine," she said, blowing her nose.

"No, I don't think it is. What's going on Morgan and what baby?"

Turning her back towards me, Morgan peered out the window. "Arthur, I don't want to talk about it."

"Yes, we are going to talk about it. I will be right back." I return to my office and pick up the phone. "Chas?"

"Yes, I'm still here."

"Listen, something is going on and I am about to find out what it is. Let me get your phone number and call you back in a few."

"Oh, okay. Is Raven alright?"

"Yes, she's fine. Morgan just got off the phone with her. What's your number?"

"Oh, good. Umm, okay, my number is 555-2695. I will wait here, by the phone, to hear back from you."

"Okay. Bye." I head back to Morgan's office to find out what has my wife so distraught. I swear, that damn Raven is a pain in the ass. She is always into some shit.

I called Stephanie over the intercom and told her to hold all of my calls and Morgan's too. I turn to the woman that I've loved for all of my life, even before I knew who she was. "Morgan, look at me. Are you pregnant?"

"Arthur, I..."

"Yes or no."

"Yes."

"How many weeks or months?"

"About twelve weeks."

Leaning against the edge of Morgan's desk, stroking my mustache, "Oh, I see," I said with a sigh. "Morgan, when were you planning to tell me?"

"Arthur, I didn't know how you would take it. I mean, I know how you feel about me having a baby with my health issues. I thought that maybe you would talk me into having an abortion."

I embrace the love of my life. "Oh Morgan, don't be silly, baby. Yes, I am very concerned with your health, but if this is what you want, then I want it too."

"Arthur, the doctor says that I am doing just fine. I have regular doctor visits and he is keeping an observation on my vitals and my internal organs. He says that my diabetes shouldn't get in the way, especially since I haven't been taking medication in over a year and have been controlling it with my diet. My doctor feels confident that I will carry our baby full-term."

"Baby, what about after you give birth? How can he assure you that you will bounce back?"

"Arthur, as a doctor, you know that he can't assure me of anything and I accept that. I believe, in my heart, that everything will be fine. The baby is not sitting on any of my organs, right now. It's going to be okay and I want you to be happy, Arthur." Morgan stroked the side of my face. "You are going to have a son."

"You know the sex already?"

"No, but I feel that it's going to be a boy."

"Baby, I want you to know that I am so happy and we will pull through this together. And, I will make a point to keep continued dialogue with your doctor. I want to know every move he makes. If I don't agree with something he does or prescribes, we are switching doctors, okay?"

"Okay, Arthur. I love you so much."

"I love you more, baby." I caress her face and enjoy the smell of her fragrance and the touch of her soft, warm lips.

"Morgan, I need to ask you something."

"Sure honey, what is it?"

"What's going on with Raven?"

"What?"

"Is everything between you and Raven okay?"

"Why do you ask?"

"Morgan, I overheard your phone conversation with Raven and you were very short with her. That is unlike you. What happened?"

"Nothing really. I am just tired of coming to her rescue. She needs to stand on her own two feet and deal with the shit she gets herself into."

"What shit, Morgan? What are you talking about?"

"It's nothing for you to worry your head over. It's just something that sisters go through every once in a while."

"It didn't sound like it to me." I searched her face for something, anything.

"Arthur, trust me. Raven is just fine."

"Well, I received a call from Chas…"

"Chas? How do you know Chas?"

"I met Chas last week when I bumped into him and Raven at the Seafood Club."

"The Seafood Club? Last week? I didn't know you went there?"

Feeling as though my ass is about to get jammed, I have to come up with a good one and fast, "Oh, yeah. The night I covered for John Howard at the hospital, I left early and stopped by there with a colleague for a drink before I picked you up," I crossed my fingers behind my back.

"Oh, okay baby. So, why did Chas call you?"

"He is concerned about Ray. He said that they had plans to meet at his place Saturday night and she never showed up. He said that he has been calling, but she won't answer the phone, and he has even gone by her place and she wouldn't answer the door."

"Well, maybe she wasn't home."

"No, he said she was home because her car was parked in the parking lot."

"Oh, well, she is probably avoiding him. You know how Ray can be when she doesn't want to be bothered."

"Now see, baby, that's what strikes me as being peculiar, because I do know how your sister can be and she doesn't strike me as someone who avoids anything or anyone. If she doesn't want to be bothered, she will let you know. Right?"

"I don't know, Arthur," Morgan replied with annoyance.

"Oh, I see. Okay, well I will call Chas back and let him know that she is safe," I said, thinking that there is much more to this than Morgan is willing to tell me. "Well, I will let you get back to work. I've got some patient files I need to review." Something is going on and I don't know what it is. Something is up with Raven, and Morgan is not letting me in on the secret. I guess I will just have to find out for myself. After locating Chas' phone number, I pick up the phone to call him back. Stephanie alerts me that Mr. Walker is on line three.

"Hi Chas, I was just about to dial your number."

"Well, what's going on?"

"Something, but, I don't know what."

"Well, what did Morgan say?"

"That's just it. She didn't say much of anything. I walked in on her while she was talking to Raven on the phone. So, at least we know that she is alive."

"Oh, well that's good. But, why won't she answer the phone?"

"I don't know, Chas. Look, this isn't any of my business, but did you two have a falling out or something?"

"No, of course not. I spoke with her twice on Saturday to confirm her coming to my place and she never came."

"Well, maybe she didn't know how to tell you that she didn't want to come over or see you or something like that."

"Arthur, I've only, personally, known Raven for a couple of weeks, but I do know of her reputation and you know as well as I do, Raven doesn't back down from anyone. If she doesn't want you, she will let you know."

"Yeah, well you do have a point."

"Arthur, something is up. I am really concerned. She won't see me or talk to me at all. Maybe she will talk to you."

"Maybe, but she and her sister are on the outs right now. I may not be a welcomed face."

"Arthur, please try."

"Okay. I will stop by Ray's place on my way home and see what I can find out."

"Great. Will you call me tonight to let me know?"

"Sure."

22 / and the award goes to...

Not being able to keep my mind on my work, I cancel all of my appointments for the afternoon. I told Morgan that I was going to hit a few balls on the range to relieve some stress. Making the drive to Raven's, I try to relax my nerves by listening to WHUR on the radio. What in the hell is going on? What is Morgan hiding? What did she mean by she was tired of cleaning up Raven's shit? I attempted to contact Raven by cell phone, hoping that if she wasn't answering the phone, she would at least check the caller ID and see that it was me calling and would pick up the phone, but no response. An eerie feeling comes over me; I do not like this whole scenario. I don't know what the hell I am in for. I call Chas on my cell. "Chas, its Arthur. Do you think you can meet me at Raven's place? I'm on my way over there now. I will wait for you in the parking lot. This whole thing is not sitting easy with me and I would prefer some back up, if you know what I mean."

"Yeah, no problem. Hey man, I think I know what's going on," Chas said, pacing the floor with a tight grip on the receiver.

"Yeah, what is it?"

"Arthur, man, I just heard on the news about a woman that was found dead in her apartment Sunday morning. The police are calling it an apparent suicide."

"Chas, I'm not following you. What does that have to do with us?"

"Arthur, the dead woman's name is Marcy Douglas."

"Okay, do you know her or something?"

"Man, I don't know. I mean, there was this chick that Raven was hanging out with all day Saturday. Man, her name is Marcy!"

"Oh my God. Do you think...?"

"Man, I don't know what to think. I hope like hell that there is no connection, for Ray's sake. Listen, I'm on my way out the door and I'll be there in fifteen minutes," Chas said, hanging up the phone, grabbing his car keys and closing the door behind him.

Trying to mentally prepare myself for whatever the hell I was in for, Morgan's phone conversation ran through my mind like wild fire. "*Ray, it is time for you to stand up and take responsibility for your actions...I am too busy trying to keep your black ass out of jail.*" Could Raven have something to do with this woman's death? What does Morgan know about all of this? When I pulled into the parking lot of Ray's complex, I saw Chas sitting in his black BMW convertible. I parked my Lexus 300 next to him.

"Hey, Chas."

"Hey man, thanks for letting me tag along. I'm just so worried about her."

"No problem, I understand. Let's just hope she opens the door for me. Have you tried to get in yet?"

"Naw, I thought I would wait for you."

"Okay, let's boogie." I closed my car door, took a deep breath and proceeded to Ray's building, with Chas on my heels.

The hallway was quiet and so were we. We knocked on the door, twice, but didn't get a response. "Raven, its Arthur, are you there?" I asked through a two-inch thick steel door. "Raven, come on baby, I know you are in there. I saw your car in the parking lot."

"Go away," came a child-like voice from the other side of the door.

"Raven, baby, it's me, Chas. Baby, please open the door. I need to see that you are okay."

"No."

"Why not, baby? Please, let us in," Chas pleaded.

"Ray, listen. If you don't open this door, I will call the police and have them knock it down."

"I'm afraid."

"Afraid of what, baby?" Chas asked.

"You may not want me anymore."

"Ray, you are talking silly. I love you baby, please let us in."

"You do?"

"Yes baby, I do. Please open the door, I need to see your face, baby." The door unlocks and Chas and I stand there, stiff as boards, with beads of sweat trickling down our face. Not from the ninety-eight-degree August heat, but from the anticipation of not knowing what awaits us on the other side of the door.

"Oh my God, baby!" Chas covers his nose with his index finger. "Baby, what in the hell..."

"Come in," she said with such a low tone of voice, we had to strain to hear her.

Chas and I stood there as though our feet were hardened in concrete. We could not believe our eyes. Raven stood before us in the same tee shirt and jeans she had on when she left Marcy's apartment. Her hair looked like a perm gone bad, with sprinkles of lint balls. Sleep was in the corner of her eyes and crust was around the edges of her mouth. She looked and smelled awful.

"I don't bite." She stepped to the side for us to enter.

"Ray, I don't understand. What is going on with you, baby?" Chas walked past his woman, thinking that a soak in a warm bath would do her just fine. The overwhelming smell of weed and funk combined, made me sick to my stomach. "Ray, you don't look so hot." I rush past her and flop on the sofa. "Why don't you have a seat and let me make sure you are okay. Chas, I believe our girl could use a nice cup of tea. Could you please take care of that for me?"

"Yeah, sure, no problem." Chas stumbled over empty beer bottles and overflowing ashtrays.

"Raven, what's wrong?"

"Nothing, I'm fine."

The smell of four-day-old funk gushes from her mouth, causing me to exhale, close my mouth and hold my breath. "Did you and Morgan have a falling out or something?" I asked through tight lips, not wanting to taste her funk. "Ray, you look like you haven't bathed in days…"

"I haven't. Didn't feel like it."

"Yes, I can smell that. At least brush your teeth."

"Why?"

"Well, it's been four days, don't you think it's time?"

"Fine." She dragged herself to the bathroom.

"Wash your ass while you're at it, babe!" Chas yelled from the kitchen.

"Kiss my ass, Chas!"

"Not until you wash that ass." Chas peeps around the corner at me with laughter dancing in his eyes and a big ass smile on his face. "The breath was kickin', huh?"

Shaking my head, "And how," I said, as we both burst into laughter.

"You both can kiss my ass, ain't shit funny." Ray said, returning to my side.

"Shut your pie hole woman, you want lemon in your tea?" Chas asked.

"Yeah, thanks."

Wiping the snot from her nose with her sleeve, "She won't talk to me."

"Why not?"

"Because."

"Because what?"

"Because."

"Morgan will not speak to you just because?"

"Yes."

"Ray, sweetie, that doesn't make any sense."

"She hates me."

"No, she doesn't hate you. She loves you."

"No, she hates me!" She pounded her fist on her knee.

"Morgan doesn't hate you. You know she's pregnant, and well, she is experiencing a lot of different emotions right now, but she doesn't hate you."

Chas searches for a clean spot on the coffee table to sit the cup of tea. With no luck, he sits the tea on the end table. Taking a seat beside her, "Raven, look at me baby. Baby, I don't like what I see. I need you to tell me what is wrong with you so that I can help you."

"No, I can't."

"Why not, baby?"

"Because."

"Because why?"

"Because."

"Ray, I need you to stop that 'because' stuff, okay baby? Now, listen to me. I am not going anywhere. I love you, Ray. Whatever it is that you are going through, we will go through it together."

"Well…" she began, glancing at Arthur for approval. "Chas, promise me that you won't get mad at me."

"I promise."

"Well…you see, it all started with Jay," she said, holding her head down from embarrassment.

"Who is Jay?" Chas asked.

"Jay is this guy I used to date a long time ago. He works in my building and I was determined to make him pay for what he did to me."

I stood at the window with my eyes fixated on her. "What did he do to you, Ray?"

"He raped me." She looked towards Chas for comfort.

"He raped you? Baby, when, where…why didn't you call the police?" Chas embraced her.

"I don't know."

"Go on." I don't believe that she is being totally upfront about the rape situation. Why didn't I ever hear anything about her being raped from Morgan?

"Because he did what he did to me, I felt that he should pay, and well I sort of set him up."

"What do you mean, baby?" Chas wonders if this pay back has anything to do with Marcy being dead.

"Well, I…I," she stumbled through her sobs and tears.

Chas looked into her eyes as though he could see the truth in them. "Ray, does this have anything to do with Marcy?"

"Huh? Marcy? Oh God." She howled like a dog in heat.

"Ray, tell me what's going on. I don't know how much more I can take of this fishing game." Chas is past the point of irritation with her.

"Okay, well, in a nutshell, I called Jay from Marcy's phone, pretending to be her, and invited him over that night, Saturday. Marcy and I were getting high and she made a move on me, and well, I didn't resist her advances. Before I knew it, we were making love on her living room floor. She took me through some experiences that I had never gone through before; fucking me with a dildo and eating my pussy." She refused to make eye contact with Chas.

"What the fuck are you saying, Raven? You had sex with another woman? What kind of shit is that?" Chas stands to his feet and begins to pace the floor.

"Hold up, Chas. Now, let's keep clear minds and open communication. Let her finish. Go ahead Ray, continue."

"Well, Marcy wanted me to put on the dildo and do her and I did. But, I might have gotten carried away. Instead of regular sex, I performed anal sex on her and that's when Jay used his key, came in and saw me doing Marcy. I got my clothes and I left after that."

I can hear the mumbling of the anger rising in Chas' throat. "But, I don't get it. When I called you, you were in your car and on your way home, but you forgot your purse, so you were going back to Marcy's place, right?"

"Yes, I was, but I felt bad for putting Marcy in the middle of my beef with Jay, so I called her and asked if I could come back and talk to her. See, before I left her place the first time, I stood outside the door and I listened to Jay demean Marcy. He was treating her like shit and was beating on her, telling her to suck his black dick, instead of a black dildo, and shit like that. I went back to talk to her and to apologize. I really did feel bad about doing what I did. For a minute, I felt like I was doing it for her because he treated her like shit. But, she didn't see it that way. She felt that I had used her and she was tired of being used by people. She killed herself."

"Ray, how did she kill herself?"

"She went into the bathroom and she got in the tub and she slashed her throat, her ankles, and her wrists. She closed the bathroom door and I couldn't stop her. She wouldn't open the door. I used the dining room chair to bust in."

"Damn, but I am still confused. When I called you for the second time, you told me that you were home and was packing a few things. Why didn't you show up?"

"When you called me, I was at Marcy's place, waiting on Morgan."

"Morgan? What does Morgan have to do with this?" I interjected.

"I didn't know who to call, so I called Morgan." She looked at me with puppy dog eyes.

"So, is this why Morgan doesn't want to speak with you?" This explains why Morgan ran out the house so fast Saturday night. How could Morgan keep something like this from me? Did she not trust my reaction or something?

"Yes, and now she hates me!"

"Ray, don't worry, Morgan will come around." I feel sorry for her because she is now reaping what she had sowed.

"Chas? Do you still love me?"

"Of course, baby."

"After all of the shit that I've done, because of me, Marcy is dead. I killed her!"

Chas cradled his woman, funky ass and all. "You did not kill her, Ray. Marcy killed herself because of her own insecurities."

"But, I used her and she was so vulnerable and I didn't care. It's all my fault!"

"Well, she is gone now and there is nothing you can do about it," I said with my hands stuffed in my pockets, still standing by the window, peering out with disgust on my face.

"Arthur, that's cruel and I can't believe you said that!" Ray got up from the sofa and walked towards me. "How dare you say some shit like that? Marcy is dead! Don't you understand that? Dead!"

I turn towards Ray and peer into her eyes. "Yes, I do understand that, and I also understand that if it weren't for your selfishness, 'all-about-me' attitude and your vindictive ways, you wouldn't be weighed with guilt. I also understand that you pulled my wife into this, knowing the status of her health. So, don't you dare turn the table on me! Yes, Marcy is dead, and yes, you used her, and yes, you did everything except put the fucking razor blade in her fucking hand!" I yelled, walking towards the kitchen. "I need a fucking drink!"

Following in Marcy's footsteps, Raven darts to the bathroom and slams the door. "You are right, Arthur, it is all my fault and I don't deserve to live! How about I slash my fucking throat, wrists, and ankles like Marcy did, and then you and Morgan will never, ever have to worry about my selfish, all-about-me, vindictive ass again! How about that?" She kicked the bathroom door.

"Raven, open this goddamn door, now! This doesn't prove shit, Raven, and I have had just about enough of this shit. Open the fucking door, now!" Chas began pounding on the door. "Don't let me have to break this bitch down! Open the damn door, Raven! Fuck it, you want to kill yourself, fine! Do us all a damn favor and slit your fucking throat! I am sick of this shit, Raven! Go ahead, do it!" Chas stormed down the hallway towards the front door, stopping face-to-face with me. "Man, she is all yours. She has held my attention long enough. When she takes her bow and steps off the stage, tell her to call me." Chas slammed the door behind him. Feeling the building shake from the door slam, I contemplate following in Chas' footsteps, but I can't just leave her like this. She is my sister-in-law, for goodness sakes. I head towards the bathroom to attempt to talk to Raven, and hopefully, stop anything before it happens. Is she really acting?

"Ray, sweetie, this is Arthur. Will you please come out and talk to me?"

"Go away!"

"No, I won't go away. I want you to open the door and let's talk about this."

"What is there to talk about?"

"Changing your life around."

"It's no use, Arthur. The one person who means the world to me doesn't want to talk to me, and my man just walked out on me. What else is there left to live for?"

"Raven, you are talking stupid. Maybe Chas was right. It's time to take your bow and step down from the stage. You no longer have an audience." I turn and walk towards the front door. "You are on your own."

"Who the hell do you think you're talking too? This is my damn house!" Raven flung the door open, knocking a hole in the wall with the doorknob and charged at me.

"Well, if that was all that it took to bring you back to your senses, I should've done it an hour ago."

"I never left my senses, just feeling depressed."

"Ray, I want you to realize that what Marcy did had nothing to do with you. We cannot hold ourselves accountable for other people's actions. We can only accept responsibility for our own."

"I know and I have. It's my fault that she is dead. I mean, Arthur, everything that Morgan said was right. I am selfish and I don't think about anyone, but myself. I want to change that about myself."

"And you can."

"How?"

"Well, you've already taken the first step, by acknowledgement."

"Chas is upset with me, huh?"

"Yeah, but if he loves you like he says he does, give him time and he will come around. He was very worried about you, Ray."

"What am I going to do about Morgan?"

"Don't worry about Morgan. Understand that her hormones are running wild, which explains why she's been biting my head off lately. But, she will come around and I know, first hand, that she thinks the world of you and you are all that she has. So, give her some space. Things will work themselves out with Morgan."

"Arthur, thank you."

"For?"

"For being the best brother-in-law in the world. I love you!" She wrapped her arms around my neck and kissed me on the cheek.

"Well, I am flattered and I love you too, Ray. Now, feeling better?"

"Yes, I do."

"Good. Now that you feel better, you need to smell better. How about a shower?" I said, pointing towards the bathroom.

"Do I smell that bad?" She smelled her armpits. "Oh my, I do smell kinda tart."

"Yeah, and you look even worse!"

"Yeah, well, I guess I need to do something about that, huh?"

"It would help."

"Arthur?"

"Yes?"

"You know, I never knew that you were so easy to talk to. But you are a great listener."

"Yeah, well, after living with your sister, trying to get a word in, is damn near impossible. So, I've learned how to be a listener instead of a respondent."

"Well, you ain't never lied! Look, I have something else I need to get off my chest, if you don't mind."

"Sure, what's up?"

"Well, it's about Chas. He said he loved me and I don't know whether to believe that or not. I know you don't know him, but it's only been a few weeks, and from the short time that you've been around him today, do you think he is sincere?"

"Well, I can tell you from a man's point of view that the "L" word is not something that men just toss around. We don't say it, if we don't mean it."

"But, we haven't even did the nasty yet. Well, not really."

"How can you 'not really' have sex? Either you did or you didn't."

"Okay, between me, you and these four walls, I was involved in a threesome with Chas and Ramone…"

"Ramone?"

"Yeah, Ramone. I don't believe you've ever met him. Ramone and I have been kicking it for about three years now. Well, we used to anyway. I haven't seen Ramone, since Chas told me that he is married. What's wrong Art, you look like you've just seen a ghost? Is my breath still kicking?"

"Raven, I feel I need to tell you something and it may put my life in jeopardy, but I feel you need to know."

"What is it?"

"Remember the night I bumped into you and Chas at the Seafood Club?"

"Yes, I remember. You were just leaving; something about having a drink with a colleague before you picked up Morgan from the office."

"Yeah, well...I don't know how to say this, Raven."

"Just say it."

"A few weeks ago, I met this woman at Roscoe's. She approached me and struck up a conversation with me. We had dinner and that was it. Well, at least I thought that was it. I couldn't stop thinking about her. Believe me, I would never intentionally do anything to hurt Morgan. I love my wife, but I guess curiosity got the best of me..."

"And?"

"Well, that evening you saw me at the Seafood Club, I had just finished having dinner with her. During that dinner, she told me some things about herself and her marriage. Raven, the woman I had dinner with was Renee Jarvis."

"Renee Jarvis? Who is that?"

"Ramone's wife. Raven, she knows all about you, where you live and about the time you and Ramone were having sex on your balcony."

"What? I..."

"Ray, she has the condom that Ramone tossed over the balcony into the bushes. She has proof and she is going to use it against him. I am sorry that I had to tell you that, but you said Chas told you, and well, I just couldn't keep it from you," I said, lowering my head and staring at the potato chip crumbs on the carpet."

"I don't know what to say."

"You don't need to say anything or do anything, Raven. Listen, sweetie, you have a wonderful man in Chas. He cares for you deeply, don't fuck that up by getting revenge on Ramone. Just let Ramone go. It's not worth ruining what you are trying to build with Chas."

"Yes, I know, but for three years, that motherfucker has been in and out of my fucking bed and fucking me into comas, and not once did he tell me that he was married! I mean, he knows everything about my life and me! I kept nothing from him. I shared my innermost feelings with him, shit that I never shared with Morgan, because I felt that we had a bond. That motherfucker!"

"Ray, be honest. If you knew he was married, would you have still let him into your life?"

"Well, I must admit, Ramone knew exactly how to love me. He knew how to take my mind, body and soul to another level. Shit, I almost got kicked out of this place because he fucked me in the hallway!"

"Okay, that is more than I need to know" I blushed, trying my best not to picture Morgan's sister in a compromising position in the hallway for the world to see, "I don't need a mental picture, Ray."

"Sorry, but, to answer your question, had Ramone fessed up about his wife after we'd made love? Yes, I would've continued see him."

"Why? Why on earth would you want someone else's husband?"

"Because Arthur, there is only one you and you are already spoken for," she said with a warm smile. "Now, get out of here and let me clean myself up. I am beginning to smell my own ass."

23 / curtain call

I've always loved this view. That's what sold me, not the realtors' constant blabbering about the wonderful location. It was the breathtaking view of the Washington Monument in all its glory, flanked by the Jefferson and Lincoln Memorials with the Capitol in the background. When I feel I need calming, all I have to do is look out my window at the Cherry Blossoms, people jogging around Haines Point, and paddle boating on the Potomac River. Although, I don't know why anyone, in their right mind, would want to paddle a damn boat on water that has an odor that leaves much to be desired. During the summer months, when it is over ninety-five degrees, I have to keep my windows closed because I can't stand the stench that waifs from that damn water. But, not even the most beautiful view I've ever seen can change how I am feeling right now.

Turning to look at the photograph of Ramone and me, that was taken at last year's Jazz Festival, I knock that sonofabitch on the floor. Who the fuck does Ramone think he is, fucking around with my feelings like that? I don't care what Arthur says about not getting revenge on Ramone. Fuck that shit, his fucking ass is mine. I am not the one to fuck with and Ramone knows this shit! In the back of my mind, I always knew something wasn't right with his ass. I didn't even have a damn home phone number. Sure, I could page him and call him on his cell whenever I wanted to. And believe me, I called that brother many late nights, and within an hour, his ass was at my front door, ready to turn my ass out.

What kind of a woman is his wife to allow that shit? Damn, if he was my husband, I would be on his ass like stank on shit, if he left out the fucking house at midnight and didn't bring his ass back until two days later! Hell, her shit ain't fresh either. That bitch, sitting at bars and picking up men, married men at that. Damn, it's still hard to believe that Arthur almost strayed. But hell, men will be men. They think with their dicks any damn way, just like Jay, and now Ramone. I can't believe Ramone's wife has been to my place! I bet it was her ass who slashed my fucking tires last summer. That was the same time that Ramone came over here and fucked me on the balcony. Shit, I will never forget that day, amongst the other days that he surprised me with some crazy shit. I swear, that brother is off the chain, which is why my ass is hooked. Well, I was hooked.

Shit, I ain't fooling nobody but myself. That man makes me weak in the knees. There isn't a man alive that can suck my clit the way Ramone can. Hell, I don't even know if Chas has mastered the art of clit sucking. The last time I fucked Chas was during that threesome with Ramone, and even then, he didn't suck the clit. But, he sure as hell was ramming that dick down my throat. Oh well, I do plan to see what Chas has to offer. I have never been with a man who makes me feel the way he makes me feel. Yeah, Ramone be tearing up the pussy, but there is something different about Chas.

When I'm with Chas, I don't even think about sex and that's odd for me because I stay horny. But, how can he love me and he ain't even tapped it yet? Hell, I am crazy about Chas, but before I go any further, I need to see what he has to offer me sexually. Fuck what you heard, I need my man to be able to fully satisfy me with his dick as well as his mouth. I don't do that partial shit.

Reaching in the linen closet for two towels, a washcloth and a scented candle, I head towards the bathroom to start my shower. Arthur was right, my ass is funky. Damn, I can't believe Chas came through my door holding his damn nose. That was some funny shit, though. It took all I had to maintain myself and continue to play the role of 'poor old Raven.' Yeah Chas, I am taking my bow right now, baby.

After testing the water temperature, I reach for the shampoo and conditioner. Stepping into the shower, I think about how Chas' anger really turned me on. It's something sexy about a man who stomps around when he doesn't get his way. Immersing myself from head to toe under the stream of water, I lather my body, beginning with my neck, working my way down my breast, stopping to massage my nipples between my fingers. Damn, this feels good and I haven't had any dick since that fucking dildo. Damn, that was some good shit.

I never thought sex with a woman would be so intense and sensual. I must admit, I did get a rush from fucking Marcy in the ass. Hell, she liked that shit too. Maybe I will get me one of those strap-on dildo today. A girl should never be without one.

The thought of Marcy's lily white ass in my face and me having control over her asshole causes me to stroke my clit, inserting my middle finger inside myself. Thinking about Chas and wanting him on my clit, I reach for the removable showerhead and turn it to pulsating. Spreading my legs, I allow the water to have its way with me.

With an orgasm building inside me, I stroke my breast and squeeze my nipple between my fingers. The urge of having to piss overwhelms me. Leaning against the shower wall, I brace myself for one hell of an orgasm. I place the showerhead closer to my clit to intensify the urge to pee. Not being able to hold it any longer, I release my urge and cum all over the showerhead. Damn, I need to call Chas. After drying myself off and allowing my hair to air dry, I dial Chas' *home* phone number. "Hi Baby!" I said with enthusiasm.

"Hey, how you doing?"

"I'm fine."

"That's good to hear." He doesn't sound too happy to hear from me.

"Chas?"

"Yeah?"

"You're mad at me, aren't you?"

"I was, but I am glad to hear your voice. You had me really worried."

"You really do care about me, don't' you?"

"More than you realize."

"But, it's only been a couple of weeks."

"And? My heart doesn't know what time it is, Ray."

"I know. Chas?"

"Huh?"

"I'm sorry."

"Sorry for what? You didn't do anything to me."

"Yes, I did. I acted stupid and immature and I didn't allow you to be there for me when you wanted to be." I sure hope he is buying this bullshit 'cause I desperately need to be fucked by a man and not a damn dildo tonight.

"Apology accepted. Look, let's just put this all behind us and move on, okay?"

"Sure baby, that sounds good to me!"

"So, what are you up to?"

"Well, I am up to trying to see my man tonight. Do you think that is possible?"

"You sure you are up for it?"

"Oh yeah, I'm sure. So, will you come over tonight?"

"How about you come over here? I think you need to get out and get some air, don't you?" He hoped that she would agree because he couldn't stomach the stench of her place tonight.

"Yeah, okay baby. Can I pack an overnight bag?"

"Sure. That would be fine."

"Good! What time do you eat me?"

"That depends."

"On what?"

"On whether or not you washed your ass!"

"That's not funny, Chas!" I laughed.

"I know baby and I'm sorry. But damn, your ass was foul today," he said in between taking gasps of air.

"Well, I just got out of the shower and I washed my hair too…on both heads. So, I am fresh, clean and ready to be your main course."

"Umm, is there something else you need to tell me, baby?"

"No, why do you ask?"

"Well, I prefer my woman to have one head and a pussy!" He laughed so hard he sounded as though he was about to pass out.

"Kiss my ass fool, you know what the hell I'm talking about. Make jokes if you want, but you gone eat some pussy tonight."

"Oh, so it's gonna be like that tonight, huh?"

"Get your knife and fork ready! You must be starved!"

"Girl, you are a fool. Yes, I could use a little something to munch on."

"See you around eight o'clock?"

"Yes, that's a good time."

"Okay baby, gotta go get myself ready!"

"Okay, and Raven?"

"Yes, Chas."

"I really do love you and I intend to show you just how much."

"I love you too." Damn, was I still on the stage?

24 / a woman scorned

Morgan insisted on painting the walls in my home office chocolate brown. Her claim for doing so was that this color calmed the nerves. And, as always, she was right—to a point. It's not so calming in here when the sun sets and I have to turn on the ceiling light and all four lamps in order to see what the hell I'm doing. But she meant well, and Morgan has always had great taste when it came to decorating. My chocolate walls are adorned with colorful artwork and brass candle sconces that have never been lit. Something about having a flame that close to the wall makes me picture this three hundred and fifty thousand dollar investment going up in flames and that scares me. Besides, Morgan doesn't want candle wax to drip on the pure white, plush wall-to-wall carpeting that she had to have all over the house. I wish we could be like regular folks and not have to take off our shoes when we walk through the front door. I think it's embarrassing to open the door and ask your guests to take off their shoes before they come any further. We are not Japanese.

As much as I try, Morgan insists on cleaning this big house without any assistance from a cleaning company. We have yet to have the carpet cleaned, but I am sure that when the time comes, Morgan will be doing that herself also. Come to think of it, she painted the upstairs bedrooms and my office. I am definitely a lucky man. But now that she is having our baby, I will insist that she does nothing. I have already placed a call to a cleaning service who will come in once a month and clean, while Morgan stands over them like a slave driver, making sure they don't miss a spot. She will not like it, but I can't take any risks with this pregnancy.

Being pregnant, with diabetes, is nothing to play around with. I know she hasn't had any diabetic episodes going on two years now, and she no longer takes her medication. But I still can't take any chances. She definitely will not like me cutting her hours at the office either. Instead of her working at the office five days a week, it will be two days a week. If she must do something, she can do it from home. I won't take no for an answer. She will give me my pants back.

Admiring the painting on the wall, trying to figure out why anyone would paint a pear that has a booty hole with a bird perched in front, I contemplated how to approach Morgan with the topic of her sister and this Marcy Douglas woman. I need to make sure that this apparent suicide was just that and nothing more. Flipping through my rolodex, I locate the number of a college friend who is now a Sergeant on the metropolitan police force.

"Sixth district, Officer Quick here," came from someone who was obviously working during his lunch, because he sounded as if he had a mouth full of something.

"Yes, I would like to speak with Sergeant Martin, please."

"Sure, just a sec." The officer yelled for Martin to take a call on line seven.

"Martin, may I help you?"

"Hey Mike, Arthur Carrington here, long time no see."

"Hey Arthur. Hell yeah it's been a long time."

"Yeah man. How are you?"

"Oh, I can't complain. Life is good. Hey, how's Morgan and the practice?"

"The practice is great and Morgan is carrying around our bundle of joy."

"Get out! Hey man, congratulations!"

"Thanks Mike, I appreciate that. Hey, how are Leslie and Paul?"

"Man, she's doing good. Still bitching about everything under the sun. Man, she just tore up the damn Nissan 300zx. For the life of me, I can't figure out how she keeps driving into those damn potholes! She has an attitude with me now 'cause I told her that her ass can't drive," he chuckled. "Paul is doing great. He's an entrepreneur now."

"Really? That's great!"

"Yeah, he's got a spot down on Rhode Island Avenue called GOTO Sports. You should check it out when you get a chance. You know, we all need to get together and have dinner or something real soon."

"Yeah, that would be nice. I'm sure Morgan would like to see Leslie. You know they are so much alike."

"Oh? Morgan bitching and complaining too?"

"Even more so now that she is pregnant. Her hormones are going to make me look for shelter elsewhere, until the baby is born."

"I hear that. So, what do I owe the honor of this call, Doc?"

"Well, I know that I am about to slightly betray my oath, but I wanted to know where things stand with the Marcy Douglas case."

"Yeah? Why is that?"

"Her father is my patient and I'm concerned about his health."

"Oh, I see. Well, her father didn't kill her if that's what you want to know."

"I didn't think he did, I just wanted to know if it is a closed case."

"Oh, and why is that?"

"Look man, could you not talk to me like the great Sergeant that you are and more like my Omega Psi Phi frat brother? I'm concerned about my patient. Of course he took his daughters death pretty hard and he looks to me for counseling…"

"I didn't know counseling was a part of the urology department."

"Counseling my patients, period, is a part of my department. Listen, sorry I bothered you. You take care," I said, obviously sounding perturbed with this asshole.

"Alright. Sorry man, but you know, I have to question any and all inquiries."

"Yeah, it's cool, but thanks anyway. I appreciate the help you didn't give me."

"Alright man, don't go getting your briefs in a knot," Mike laughed. "The case is closed. Marcy Douglas committed suicide. Her slashed body was found in her bathtub, naked with a dildo in her hand."

"Oh my God! That's horrible. No wonder my patient is so upset. I would be too if I found my daughter like that."

"Who says the father found her?"

"No one, I was just saying."

"Yeah, well, from what we gathered, she had a, shall we say, freaky lifestyle. That chick had dildos in all sizes, shapes and colors. Not to mention she was a regular up on the row."

"The row?"

"Yeah, you know, 14th and U Streets."

"Oh, I see. And you are sure she committed suicide?"

"Yeah, we are sure. There were no other fingerprints around and no signs of forced entry or the possibility of other people being involved. The place was spotless. Need any more information to help counsel your patient?"

"Nope, that will do it. Listen, thanks man, I really appreciate your help. Hey, when was the last time you had a check up?"

"Why?"

"Well, if it's been a while, you need to come and see me, on the house, of course."

"Hell no, man. If anybody is going to be sticking their finger up a brother's asshole, it sure as hell won't be you!"

"Yeah, I hear you. Listen, take care and if you ever need anything, you know where to find me."

"Yep, sure do. Give Morgan my love and don't be a stranger. Call a brother every now and then, just for GP."

"Okay, I will do that, and give my love to Leslie and tell her to ease up off those pot holes. Bye now."

Putting two and two together, I come to the conclusion that the reason Marcy's place was spotless is because Morgan performed her magic. I can just picture it now. Ray scared out of her mind, calls Morgan for help. Morgan goes over there and throws out cleaning instructions from the time that she steps through the door. Morgan probably got fed up with Raven and showed a side of herself that Raven didn't know existed. Well, the case is closed and that's a good thing. Now, I've got to find a way to bring Morgan and Raven back together. Morgan isn't fooling anyone, but herself. I can see through the façade. She misses her sister. Ready to call it a night and spend quality time with my wife, my pager sounds off with a number that I am not familiar with. It must be a patient. The only time my pager goes off at this time of the evening is when a patient calls the office and is redirected to my answering service.

"This is Dr. Carrington, returning a call from this number."

"Hello Arthur, I was hoping you would return the call."

"Renee?" Damn she has caller ID and is probably writing down my home office number as we speak.

"Yep. You miss me?"

"I beg your pardon? What can I do for you, Mrs. Jarvis?"

"Enough with the formalities. We are on first name basis, remember?

"Mrs. Jarvis, is this call of a medical nature?" I made myself very clear at the restaurant that I was not interested in a fling or anything of the sort. What is she trying to pull?

"Yes, I need my Dr. Feel Good," she said with a giggle.

"Renee, listen, this is not cool. Not cool at all. I am going to have to end this call. Take care."

"Arthur, wait! Please, I want to see you. I need to see you. I don't want to go through life wondering what it would have been like being with you," she pleaded.

"Renee, I don't know any other way to make it clear to you, I love my wife. I should not have called you and invited you to dinner, that was wrong. But, there was no harm done and I would like for us to leave it just as it was meant—a friendly dinner between associates."

"Associates? Oh, I see. You make a move on me, get scared and now you don't want to continue what you started."

"No, I didn't start anything. As a matter of fact, I ended us before anything could get started."

"You listen to me Dr. Arthur Carrington, I don't know who you think you are. Do you think you can just walk into my life and walk out when you get ready?"

"Okay, I think this call has gone on long enough."

"No, I don't think so! I wonder what your little pregnant wife would think about you having dinner with another woman that you picked up in a bar?"

"First of all, you approached me. Secondly, I had dinner with an associate and that is it."

"Now come on Artie, do you really think wifey is going to believe that bullshit?"

"Well, what would Mr. Jarvis think about you having dinner with another man?"

"Mr. Jarvis doesn't give a rat's ass if I fucked all of Washington, D.C., so long as he can continue to fuck that Raven bitch! Besides, I found me a real man in you and I intend to hear the beautiful music that you and I would make."

"Okay, enough is enough. You obviously have preconceived notions about us and I am sorry, but they will never come to fruition. Now, I will have to end this call. Take care and please, have a nice life."

"Yeah, whatever Doc. But trust me, you haven't heard the last of me. I will have you, Arthur. I will!" she yelled, before slamming the phone in my ear.

With the receiver still in my hand, my feet are frozen where I stand. I can't move. My body is numb. Is this what it feels like when someone threatens to stalk you? Placing the receiver into its cradle, I fall back into my leather ergonomic desk chair that Morgan said I had to have because of my back problems. Staring at the wall, I contemplate making it easier on myself by telling Morgan everything. She will never understand that I briefly lost my senses. Plus, as soon as I tell her, she will pick up that damn phone and call that crazy ass Raven. Damn, why didn't I think of her in the first place? I can call Raven. I've already told her what went down with Renee anyway. Maybe she can help me out of this mess. After all, getting in and out of mess is Raven's specialty. Shoot, calling Raven would be the same as telling Morgan. Hell, I might as well cut out the middle man, or in this case, the middle woman and just tell her myself. Yeah, that is the best thing to do. Gathering up the nerve to approach Morgan, I can smell the steaks cooking on the grill. Maybe I will tell her after dinner, while she is not around the cutlery set. Turning off the lights and closing down the home office for the evening, my office phone rings.

"Dr. Carrington."

"Guess who?"

"Renee, my patience is running very thin with you right now. It's late, I am tired and I am not in the mood for your childish antics."

"See, you guessed it! And they said you weren't smart," she giggled.

"Renee, I am trying to remain calm with you. I would appreciate you never calling me again."

"If I do, whatchu' gone do 'bout it? Not a goddamn thing, that's what. You picked up the wrong woman this time, Dr. Do Right. So, why don't you make it easy on yourself and your little wifey and meet me tonight. I promise to make it worth your while and you will be back home with that bitch of yours before the sun comes up."

"You listen to me, you whore. Don't fuck with me or my family, you got that tramp? No, you picked up the wrong man, this time. Trust me, you fuck with my family and I will fuck with yours." I slammed the phone in its cradle.

Standing in the door, "Honey, what's going on?" Morgan asked, scaring the shit out of me.

"Baby, how long have you been standing there?"

"Long enough to hear you threaten to fuck up someone's family. What is going on, Arthur?"

"Morgan, it is nothing for you to worry about, just some prank caller."

"On your office phone? I thought it was unpublished? How did they get your number?"

Seeing that she is getting herself worked up, I try to calm her down. "Morgan, you listen to me. There is absolutely nothing for you to worry about. It was a prank caller. As a matter of fact, it sounded like a child playing on the phone. His parents are probably out for the evening and he is randomly dialing phone numbers and playing tricks on people. You know, just like we used to do when we were kids."

"Yeah, Ray and I used to pick people out of the phone book and call them and ask them if their refrigerator was running, and when they would say yes, we would yell 'you better go catch it!'" she laughed. "You know Arthur, you're probably right."

"Baby, speaking of Ray, why don't you give her a call? I can see in your eyes that you miss her."

"Yes, I do miss her, but I can't call her right now."

"Why not, baby?"

"Because Raven is a selfish bitch and I have no room in my life for that kind of foolishness. I have my health and my baby to worry about. I can't take the stress that comes with her right now. You wouldn't understand, Arthur."

"Yes, I do understand. I know what is going on."

"What do you mean?"

"I know about Marcy Douglas."

"Oh Arthur, how did you find out?"

"Chas and I went to see Raven today. She told me everything."

"She told Chas too?"

"Yep. You know how your sister can be. She put on a good act. And well, Chas seems to be a pretty smart guy. When Ray locked herself in the bathroom and refused to come out, he stormed out and didn't come back."

"Damn, she locked herself in the bathroom? See, I told you that girl comes with nothing but drama and stress. I don't know why she is that way. She wasn't like that when we were kids. I just don't know, Arthur."

"Well, she also told me that she called you and you came over. Now, she didn't go into details, but knowing my wife like I do, you cleaned that place up, didn't you?"

"Just a teensy bit," she said, making the size gesture with her thumb and index finger. "But, I couldn't see her go to jail for something that she didn't do."

"Well, not physically anyway."

"What do you mean?"

"Well, while Ray didn't have razor in hand and she didn't slice up home girl, she did play a role in pushing her to that point."

"Yeah, you're right. I just don't know what I'm going to do with her."

"You will allow her to clean up her own mess, that's what you will do. Baby, Ray is a grown woman. She has to take responsibility for her actions, plain and simple."

"I know baby, but I can't see my sister in jail."

"You won't. I put in a call to Mike Martin and he assured me that the Marcy Douglas case was closed. She committed suicide and there were no fingerprints found anywhere. As a matter of fact, the place was spotless. I wonder whose handy work that was?" I admired the glow in my wife's face. Morgan is so beautiful. I can't believe I thought about stepping out on her. I am glad I came to my senses. I don't ever want to imagine how life would be without her.

"Well, that's good. Listen, all of this talking is making me hungry. The steaks are ready, let's eat."

"I doubt if the talking is what's making you hungry. It's probably my son you're toting around in your belly," I chuckled.

"Yeah, and this little rascal has me sick as a dog in the mornings." She patted me on my cheek. "I love you, Arthur."

"I love you too, baby. Now look, you go on and get things ready and let me finish up in here. I'll be out shortly."

"Okay, but hurry up 'cause I'm hungrier than a hostage."

"I bet you are. Close the door behind you, baby," I chuckled. Without a thought, I pick up the phone and dial Ray's number. "Ray, its Arthur."

"Hey Arthur, what's up?"

"You're sounding much better."

"I feel much better."

"Good. Listen, I need to discuss something with you and it must stay between us, okay?"

"Sure, what's up?"

"I am serious, Ray. This cannot get back to Morgan. I don't want anything causing her or the baby any stress. She doesn't need that right now."

"Okay, what's up?"

"Renee Jarvis called me this evening."

"You gave her your home phone number? Damn, and these no good fuckers I've been dealing with only give me a damn pager or cell number."

"No, of course not, but she does have it."

"Umm, okay. You wanna tell me how she got the damn number? I know she didn't pull that bitch outta thin air."

"She called my office, after hours, and the answering service paged me. I called the number back, thinking that it might have been a patient or something. Well, I guess she has caller ID or she did that *69 thing, because just as I am standing here talking to you, she called me back."

"Damn, that's one bold ass bitch. Okay, so what you want me to do about it? After all Arthur, you didn't think with the right head, if you know what I mean."

"Ray, nothing happened between us, and yes, I do know what you mean."

"Okay, so if nothing happened, then why is she calling you? Besides, I thought you ended it at the restaurant. That is what you told me, right?"

"Yes, I did, but she won't take no for an answer. She even threatened to tell Morgan if I don't see her."

"Yeah, well, you are in a tough spot, aren't you?"

"Yes I am and I was hoping that maybe you could help me out."

"Help you out, how?"

"Raven, you aren't talking to some thug you just met on the street. I know you and I know that since I told you about Renee being Ramone's wife, you are plotting something in that pretty little head of yours."

"Arthur, you don't know shit."

"Oh? Tell me I'm wrong."

"Alright, damn. Okay, so what role do you want me to play?"

"I want you to get her off my back."

"I don't know how I am going to do that, Arthur. Once a woman has her mind set on getting a man, nothing will stand in her way."

"Raven, she threatened Morgan."

"Hold up. That bitch threatened my sister?"

"Yes."

"Oh, it's on now."

"Good," I said with a sigh of relief. "What do you have planned?"

"Hmm, let me think about it. Whatever the plan, you are definitely going to do your part, since this shit is your fault."

"Yeah, whatever you want me to do. We just can't let Morgan find out. It would kill her, and not to mention, our marriage."

"She won't find out. Now, let me think about it. I will call you tomorrow. I am on my way to see Chas."

"Yeah? Chas is a nice guy. He really does care for you, Ray. Don't fuck it up!" I said with laughter.

"Whatever. I'll call you tomorrow."

25 / he loves me, he loves me not...he loves me!

Well, it's eight o'clock and no Raven. Damn, if she stands me up again, this will be the end of her. I opened up my heart too soon. I can't believe I told her that I loved her. That is not a word that I typically throw around, but I can't stop thinking about her and wanting her. I guess I do love her, seeing as though I haven't tried to bed her yet. And, knowing the type of woman Ray is, I am surprised she hasn't made a move on me. Maybe she's saving it all for Ramone. Damn, I hope she isn't still wrapped up in him. He has it all; a beautiful wife, two adorable kids and a wonderful home. Why would he go and fuck that up? I don't get it. Brothas are always saying that there are no good women around. As soon as they get one, they fuck over her, which makes me totally understand how black women can have bitterness for black men. We are straight dogs, but I try to play things differently. Hell, I treat a woman, black or white, with respect because that is how I want to be treated in return.

Pacing the living room floor, hoping that Raven doesn't pull a disappearing act, I check on dinner. I wanted to surprise her with her favorite foods. She loves crab, so I prepared Crab Stuffed Portobellas for an appetizer and Crab Imperial for the entrée. She deserves it. My baby has been through a lot. Now typically, I would serve a Chardonnay, but since my girl loves her brandy, I will have to save the Chardonnay for another day. Carrying the plates to the dining room table, my phone rings.

"Chas? It's Arthur."

"Hey Arthur, 'sup man?"

"Not much. Just wanted to call you and thank you for being there for Raven. Morgan and I really appreciate you doing that."

"Hey man, that's my lady. I will always be there for her until she tells me to go away for good." I chuckled. "Does Morgan know what happened today?"

"Yeah, I had to break down and tell her. She handled it fine. Although, let her tell it, she could care less. But, I can see in her eyes that she misses

Raven. Hell, I miss Raven. Instead of Morgan running her mouth on the phone with her sister, she's talking my damn ear off man."

"Yeah man, I had no idea that Ray could talk the way she does. But you know, I really don't mind it either. I mean, her conversations are intelligent. I can talk to Ray about anything. She has her views on everything and it is so stimulating to have a decent conversation with a woman. You know what I mean?"

"Yeah, I know what you mean. Both she and Morgan can be very opinionated. Well, I just got off the phone with Ray, I know she is headed your way so I won't hold you. Listen, you play golf?"

"Golf? Naw man. The closest I've gotten to a golf course is living vicariously through Tiger Woods!"

"Well listen, it's fun and it's easy and you can make a lot of good contacts. By the way, what's your profession, if you don't mind me asking?"

"Naw, not at all. I'm an Investor. I buy and sell real estate."

"Yeah? Very lucrative business."

"Sure is."

"How about me and you hook up one Saturday and head to the course? I can teach you how to play golf and you can give me pointers on buying and selling real estate."

"Sounds like a plan to me. Listen man, I've gotta check on dinner…"

"Dinner? Oh no! Man, you cooking dinner for Ray?"

"Yeah, what's wrong with that?"

"Nothing. You just making the rest of us look bad, that's all!" he said with uncontrollable laughter. "I will holler at you later. Peace."

Since Arthur confirmed Ray's attendance, I can finish preparing for what I hope to be an evening full of passion and some good fucking, because my dick is rock hard like a motherfucker! Looking at my watch, the big hand is on the six and the little hand is on the eight and why the hell can't women get anywhere on time. Walking towards the bedroom, the phone rings.

"Hi baby."

"Hey you, are you coming this way any time soon?"

"Well, as soon as you open the door."

Hanging up the phone, I sprint down the stairs to open the door for my lady.

"Raven, what the hell…!" I exclaimed. "Woman, where are your damn clothes?"

"In my bag. It's kind of breezy out here. Step to the side sexy, I don't want to catch cold." She walked in my house, ass naked, wearing only a pair of three-inch, come-fuck-me pumps. Damn, she is just full of surprises!

"Raven, my God! Did you drive over here naked?"

"No, I walked the twenty miles. Of course I drove, Chas."

"Naked?"

"Yep."

"Oh, hell no. I don't want my woman out in public, ass naked, for every motherfucker to get a hard on!" I said, raising my voice.

"Calm down, Chas. I have tinted windows, remember?"

"Woman, you are crazy as shit. Suppose you would have gotten pulled over by the cops or gotten into an accident or something?"

"Well, I didn't. So, calm down. I swear, you're the only man I know that gives his woman grief because she shows up at his door naked instead of taking her and fucking her brains out."

"Well damn, you just caught me off guard with this shit. Besides, I didn't want to jump your bones as soon as you walked through the door. I have plans."

"Oh, you do?"

"Yes, I do…but damn woman. You have the most beautiful, flawless body I've ever seen." I walked towards her.

She takes a step back, turning around and walking that nice, round ass towards the living room sofa. "Thank you and it's all right here for you to do whatever your heart desires." Walking behind her, I feel my dick rising to the occasion. "Baby, I want you to sit right there," she said, pointing towards the sofa as she sashays over to the leather winged-backed chair, taking a seat and spreading her legs. Right before my eyes, Raven begins to masturbate. Trying to maintain my cool, I lean back on the sofa and watch her put on the best performance yet. "Come here, Chas. I want you over here, on your knees, in front of my pussy."

Walking towards her, I unzip my jeans. Kneeling before her, the smell of her sweetness overwhelms me and I begin to ravish her, tasting her and stroking her clit with my tongue. The doorbell rings, "Damn, who the hell can that be?"

"Don't answer it, baby?"

Ignoring the uninvited guest, I continue to suck on her clit, feeling it begin to swell between my lips. The doorbell rings again, "Damn, that fucking doorbell is fucking up my concentration. Ray, let me see who is at the door."

"No! Fuck 'em. Don't stop, baby!"

"Baby, I can't focus on you with that fucking doorbell ringing like that. I will only be a minute. Let me get rid of whoever it is. Stay put." I stood up, attempting to adjust the hard-on in my pants. "On second thought, why don't you go upstairs. I don't want anyone to see my baby spread eagle like that."

"Fuck whoever it is. Shit, fucking up my groove."

"I know baby, but please go upstairs. For me?"

"Okay, but don't be too long." She walked past me and up the stairs. "Oh, by the way, there is a nice warm bath waiting for you."

"Hmm, sounds yummy. Hurry up, baby." I watched as that firm, round ass of hers glide up the stairs. Watching her causes my dick to try and fight it's way through my jeans. Before opening the door, I adjust my dick again.

"Hey man, 'sup? Long time no see!"

My dick deflates at the sight of Ramone. Standing in the doorway, I let my body do the talking. "Yo, man. Yeah, it's been a long time. What's up man? What brings you by?"

"I just stopped by. Haven't heard from you in a while. I stopped by Ray's place to hang out with her, but she wasn't home. So, I thought you and I could hang out and do something."

"Well, sorry man, I can't tonight. I have a lady visitor."

"Word?"

"Yeah man."

"Damn, who is she? Do I know her? Damn man, I can't believe you kept this shit from me. How long yall been kickin' it?"

"Well, we just hooked up and I don't think you know her. Listen man, thanks for stopping by, but a brother needs to get back to takin' care of his bidness, if ya know what I mean."

"Right, right. I hear you man. Yo, knock a hole in the left side of that pussy for me. Renee ain't opening up her damn legs and Ray's ass done gone AWOL on a brother," he said, giving me dap.

"Yeah, right. Take it easy man." I closed the door before I put a hole in the left side of his fucking jaw. Before going upstairs to pick up where I left off, I pour myself a shot of brandy to calm me down. I can't believe I let that motherfucker insult my woman to my face. Damn, I felt like knocking him through the fucking wall. "Fuck!" I yelled, slamming the glass on the counter.

"What's wrong baby?" Ray yelled from the bathroom. "Is everything okay?"

"Yeah, you want a drink?"

"Yes, that would be nice." After pouring myself a second shot and taking it to head, I pour a glass for Ray and head up the stairs to the bathroom.

"Hey baby! This bath was a wonderful idea. Won't you join me?"

"Is there room?"

"Is there room? What the hell you tryin' to say?" she asked, rising up in the tub.

"Down girl."

"Well, strip Boo and come on in before the water gets too cold." She slid towards the front of the tub. Stripping down to my birthday suit, which still looks good, thanks to the mini gym I built in my basement last summer, I climb into the tub behind Ray. "Now, doesn't this feel nice?" She lays back against my chest and starts stroking my knee.

"Yeah, but I was hoping that we could pick up where we left off." I stroked her nipple with my index finger.

"We will. What's the rush? We have all night."

"You are the one who came to my door ass naked" I kissed her on her earlobe.

"You liked that, huh?"

"Yeah, it was…different. That's what I like about you, baby. You aren't like the other girls, and I use that term loosely, that I've been with."

"How so? We all have the same thing, a pussy!"

"Yeah, well, yall might have the same thing, but yall don't work that shit the same!"

"Chas?"

"Yeah baby."

"When you told me that you loved me…"

"Ray, don't you believe me?"

"Well, I guess."

"You guess? Either you do or you don't."

"No. I mean, yes. I mean…I don't know what the hell I mean. All I know is that I don't want to be hurt again. The last time I opened myself up, the motherfucker stomped all over my heart, which is probably why I am the way that I am today. And now this shit with Ramone, I am finding it very hard to trust anyone at the moment."

"How did he stomp all over your heart?"

"It's a long story, baby."

"Well, I've got plenty of time where you are concerned. I want to know what makes you tick, Ray."

"Well, a few years ago, I was dating this guy who works in my building named Jay. I was so in love with this man and I thought he felt the same. We were inseparable, we even discussed marriage. That motherfucker had me picking out colors for bridesmaid dresses. Morgan was so excited that I was going to settle down and, as she puts it, stop running the streets. Finally, we set the date. I hired a wedding coordinator, purchased my wedding gown, picked out dresses for my attendants, and hired the caterer; the whole nine yards. Everything was going to be perfect. My wedding was going to go off without a hitch and I was going to be the happiest woman in the world because I was going to marry this man that I loved more than anything in the world," she hesitated, as if needing to catch her breath.

I am intrigued by the story and finding out why Ray is the way that she is. "Well, why didn't the wedding take place?"

"Well, one day I had a doctor's appointment so I didn't get to work until late. I am standing at the elevators waiting for them to come and, you won't believe this shit, but when the elevator doors opened, I saw this woman with her legs wrapped around my man's waist, getting fucked!"

"What?"

"Yep! That dumb bastard didn't have since enough to press the OFF switch. Evidently, they were just getting started, because instead of his dick being inside her, he was finger fucking her."

"Damn baby. I am so sorry to hear that."

"Don't be sorry, baby. It wasn't your dick that was trying to find its way into that bitch."

"Damn, well I can see how that would cause you not to trust anyone."

"Yeah, and you know the part that was really a trip?"

"No, what?"

"Not only was this motherfucker engaged to me, but he was also engaged to the bitch in the elevator from the first floor, the bitch on the tenth floor and the bitch on the sixth floor!"

"What? You mean he was dating all four of you at one time and in the same damn building?"

"Yep, sure was."

"Well, how in the hell did he get away with that? I mean, how did he keep you all separate?"

"I don't know how he did it, but he did. You know that was some real playa shit too. I give him his props. He played that shit out perfectly, but I never forgave him for that."

"I can't say that I blame you. But baby, I am not Jay. I am Chas and I do love you and my intentions are to be with you for as long as you will have me." I palmed her breast and kissed her neck.

"Chas, there's more."

"Okay, shoot. It can't be worse than what you've just told me."

"Well, I don't know. Listen baby, for some reason I feel like I need to come clean with you. I want to open myself up to you, but I think I need to tell you everything before I do that. And well, if you don't want to see me after I come clean, then I will understand and I will never darken your doorstep again."

"Damn baby. Well, I can't make you any promises. Go ahead and give it to me."

"Well, you remember when you called me at my office?"

"Yeah, I remember."

"Well, after I hung up with you, I gathered my things to leave because I was really excited about us hooking up. And well, I bumped into Jay on the elevator."

"Okay. So far I still want you."

"Yeah, well, like I just told you, I never forgave him for what he did to me. So, umm, well, I made a pass at him on the elevator."

"And?"

"And, well, instead of me fucking him, he fucked me. Actually, he took me. I lost control of the situation with him, once again. I didn't like that so I was determined to get him back for that."

"Well, what does that have to do with me, Ray?"

"Well, everything. I fucked another man before hooking up with you."

"Okay, but there was no understanding between us, right?"

"Right. But…"

"And it's not like we were hooking up to fuck anyway, right?"

"Right. But…"

"And you haven't been with anyone else in the past couple of weeks since we've been hanging heavy, right?"

"Right. But…"

"There is no 'but' baby. Listen, what you did before me, is your business and your past. The only thing I care about is how your past has affected you and whether or not it will roll over into what we are trying to build."

"I understand baby, but that is only half of it."

"Okay. Well, if you must tell me, go ahead."

"Well, yes I must. I need to come clean and I need to know that, if you take me for me, I can willingly give my heart to you. Chas, I so badly want to love again and be loved, really be loved."

"Okay fine. But, the water is getting cold and I wish you would hurry up and say what you need to say so I can pick up where I left off before we were so rudely interrupted."

"Okay, the short version and to leave out the morbid details, I used Marcy to get back at Jay. That's why she killed herself, because of me and my selfishness. Morgan was right, I don't think about anyone but myself!" She began to cry.

"Baby, baby…let's get out this cold ass water." Rising up and stepping out of the tub, I wrap a towel around my waist. "Come on baby." I reached for her hand to help her get out of the tub. Wrapping a towel around her, "Baby, like I said, that is your past. You've been hurt and while I don't believe that your actions were warranted, I do understand."

Taking her face in the palm of my hands, "Raven Ward, I love you. I've always loved you and now that I have you, I am going to keep you and treat you right. That is, if you will have me. Ray, will you be my woman? Will you let me love you and cherish you?"

She gazed into my eyes with those big beautiful doe-like eyes. "Are you sure?"

"Yes, I am sure."

"Yes, I will have you." Smiling at my woman, kissing her soft lips and bringing her into me, I insert my finger into her moist pussy, giving her pleasure. Throwing her head back with moans and groans, "Chas, let's go into the bedroom."

Refusing to remove my finger, we walk from the bathroom to my bed with my finger still inside of her, stroking her G-spot. I gently lay her on the bed like a delicate porcelain doll, not wanting to break her. With her legs propped on the bed as though she was in a pair of stirrups in a gynecology office, I kneel before her sweetness, with my finger still stroking her G-spot, I begin to tickle her clit with my tongue. From the heaving of her body, I can tell that she's about to reach her climax.

"I want you inside me baby."

"Ray, does this belong to me?"

"Yes," she replied through a moan.

"Does all of it belong to me?"

"Yes!"

"I don't want another motherfucker, male or female, inside my pussy. Are we clear?"

"Yes, yes, yes!"

"Good. Now, cum for daddy," I said, adding more friction to her G-spot.

"No, I want to cum on your dick."

"Is this my pussy?"

"Yes, it's your pussy, damn!"

"Well, since it's my pussy, it will cum the way I want it to cum. Now, cum for daddy. Cum on baby, cum for your daddy." I continuously stroke her G-spot, feeling it swell, while nibbling on her clit.

"Oh God, I've gotta pee! Stop Chas, I've gotta pee!"

"No you don't," I said, still stroking her G-spot with more friction.

"What the fuck? How you gonna tell me? I should know if I have to piss or not!"

"Raven, baby, you don't have to pee. Now, do as I say and let it go."

"Let it go?"

"Yes."

"You mean you want me to piss in your face?" She propped herself up on her elbows.

"No. You won't piss in my face. You will ejaculate. What you are feeling is the need to release. Let it go."

"But Chas…"

"Do it now!"

Gazing into my eyes with confusion, she laid flat on the bed and began to fuck my finger with her pussy. "Yes baby, that's it. Give it to me baby." Lifting the hood of her clit with my index finger, I stroke under the hood with my tongue.

"Oh shit!" As her body begins to quiver, her moans and groans grow louder. "Oh baby, damn!" she yelled to the top of her lungs, as I feel her muscles tightening up around my finger and her clit swelling, looking like it is about to burst.

"Cum baby, cum for daddy. Cum for Chas baby."

Ray's body stiffens and a thick, clear substance starts to shoot all over of my face. "Oh damn! What the hell was that? I have never experienced anything like this before. I am so weak. Did I just shoot some shit from my pussy?"

"Yes, you certainly did."

"What the hell was that?"

"You ejaculated."

"Ejaculated? Baby, only men ejaculate."

"Not true, baby. Women have what is called a female ejaculation. Do I need to school your ass on that?"

"Yeah, I think you better!"

"Okay, let's climb under the sheets and I will tell you all about female ejaculations."

Pulling the covers back and sliding under them, "This should be interesting," she said.

"Female ejaculation is when a woman releases fluid from her external sex organs, combined with sex. Now, some would say that this fluid is released under pressure, like stroking the G-spot, while others say it must be combined with a woman's orgasm. Female ejaculations are very hard to find, and a brother, like myself, has to know what he is doing in order to find it. However, some say it's a myth and some say it's the gospel."

"Shit, a myth it ain't! I am living proof."

26 / i am my sister's keeper

Well, I guess I am his woman now, seeing as though he wasn't taking no for an answer. I liked that though. I like for a man to stand up and take charge, and did he take charge. I've got to admit that this brother blew my mind last night. Chas has skills. And, not only has he mastered the art of clit sucking, but he also found my G-spot. Hell, I didn't even know I had a damn G-spot. Yep, I can safely say that my ass is sprung.

I wonder who was at the door last night? It wasn't nobody, but that damn Ramone. I am sure he knew I was here, which is probably why he stopped by. Hell, my car is parked in Chas' driveway. Fuck it, I ain't got shit to hide from that married bastard. What the hell can he say to me? Nothing! Not a damn thing, which is why I ain't worried about his ass. Besides, Chas definitely replaced his ass last night.

Yeah, I am going to clean my shit up for sure. Chas is a good man and he really does care for me and I don't want to fuck that up. But, I won't sleep until I get that bastard, Ramone, back one way or another. And now, his trick ass wife is after Arthur. Nope, gotta take care of business and take care of it quick.

I wonder if Chas plans to tell Ramone about us? I should wake his ass up and ask him, but he is sleeping so peaceful. He had a sista going all night long. Hell, we didn't stop fucking until five in the morning and my shit is sore too. I have never had anyone to make me ejaculate before and three times in a row at that. Damn, it's like he knew every inch of my body. I wouldn't be surprised if Ramone told him about our escapades. Hell, you know what they say, if you brag to your friends about how good your man or woman is in the bed, when you turn your back, those so-called friends will be all up in your shit, while you are out at the grocery store or something.

I've gotta call Arthur today. Although he made a bad decision, he's still a good man. I mean, it ain't like he fucked her or anything. Having dinner really ain't all that bad, but his intentions were to fuck her and that is where he went wrong. "How am I going to handle that trick bitch?" I thought to myself. Easing out of bed, being careful not to wake Chas, I head downstairs to call Arthur. Damn, I hope Morgan doesn't answer the phone. I swear I don't feel like her bringing me down from my high.

"Morning Arthur, its Ray."

"Morning Ray. How are you?"

"I am just wonderful!"

"I bet you are."

"Shut up!"

"You want your sister?"

"Umm, no. I was calling for you."

"Okay, what's up?"

"You and I need to talk…"

"About?"

"Okay, don't play dumb. You know what about. About cleaning up your mess, that's what about."

"Yeah, that's right."

"Yeah, that's right. Has she called back since last night?"

"Yep. I turned the ringer off on my office phone, so I don't have to worry about that. But, she is having the answering service blow my pager up."

"Oh? Hmm, what number is she using? Cell or home?"

"Well, it's not her cell, so I am assuming it's her home phone."

"Damn, now that's bold. Give me the number."

"Why?"

"Do you want to get rid of this trick or what?"

"Yes, but…"

"But shit. Right now I am on Chas' phone and I can't talk. So, meet me at my place around six o'clock."

"Okay, I will be there. Want me to bring anything?"

"Arthur, we are not going to have a damn party," I said, hanging up the phone.

Making my way into the kitchen, I search the refrigerator for orange juice or something to drink. My mouth is dry and my jaws hurt. I really worked Chas last night. On a scale of one to ten, I would definitely give myself a twenty.

"Morning sweetheart," came from Chas, yawning and walking down the steps in nothing but skin.

"Morning baby. How are we this morning?"

"We are just fine." He wrapped his arms around me and kissed me on my cheek. "I rolled over and you weren't there, so I thought I would come looking for you."

"Well, you found me. I was looking for some juice or something."

"How about some breakfast?"

"Sure, but I don't see anything in your refrigerator that begins to look like sausage and eggs."

"Well, let's see. We can warm up the dinner that we didn't get around to eating last night or we can go out and grab a bite to eat. It's up to you, babe."

"Dinner? You cooked dinner?"

"Yep! But your birthday suit threw my plans off kilter."

"Damn baby, what did you fix?"

"Your favorite. Crab."

"Crab? Where's it at?"

"Probably still in the oven. But I don't think we should eat it, since it hasn't been refrigerated."

"Shit, think I won't?"

"Alright then. I hope you don't end up with the runs."

"Baby, the only thing that will be running is my tongue all over your dick as soon as I finish eating up the crab." I chuckled, smacking him on his ass.

Chas bent over to remove the Crab Imperial from the oven. I playfully smacked him on his ass. "So, what's on your agenda today?"

"Well, it is a beautiful day out," I said, looking out the huge picture window with the blinds open for all to see my natural beauty.

Chas peeked around the corner from the kitchen. "Umm, baby, do you think you could not stand in the window like that? The only eyes I want on that body are mine."

"Yeah okay, and for the record, this pussy belongs to me!"

"Yeah, whatever. Answer my question."

"What question?"

"What are your plans for today?"

"Well, I really need to clean up my place. It smells awful."

"What about this evening?"

"What, you haven't had enough?"

"I will never have enough of you baby."

"Well, I am meeting with Arthur this evening."

"Oh? Why? Wait, on second thought, that's none of my business."

"No, it's okay. If I didn't want you to know, I wouldn't have mentioned it. Arthur needs my help."

"Okay," he said, spooning the Crab Imperial onto the plates.

"I'm hungry, where's the food, Chef Chas?"

"It's coming, have a seat," he said, bringing the plates to the dining room table.

Taking my seat on the side of the table, "Oh no baby, sit here." Chas pulled out the chair at the head of the table. "My queen will sit at the head of my table." He pushed the chair under me and planted a kiss on my forehead.

Joining hands and saying grace before our meal, I can't help but to cleanse myself totally with Chas. "Baby, I need to tell you why I am meeting with Arthur," I said, realizing that I probably spoke too soon.

"Sure, what's up," he said, using his fork as a shovel.

Having second thoughts, I lie through my teeth, "Well, Arthur is trying to mend my relationship with Morgan."

"That's good. That's your sister and you two shouldn't be on the outs. You should never let anything come between you and your sister, not even me."

"Why do I feel like you are the best thing that has happened to me?"

"Because I am."

Driving home wearing Chas' gray sweat pants and tee shirt, I run a strategy plan through my mind. I've gotta make Ramone pay. He can't get away with this shit. And his trick ass wife, Renee, is fucking with my family and that shit doesn't fly with me. Since the bitch knows where I live, she should've done research on my ass and found out that I will fuck up anyone who even thinks about bringing harm to my family, especially Morgan.

Morgan is a moody ass bitch and might not want to have anything to do with me right now, but she is my sister and I love her like crazy. She will come around. I ain't worried too much about Morgan.

Morgan had to grow up fast after a drunk driver took the lives of our mama and daddy. I was ten years old and Morgan was twelve. For as long as the money rolled in, Aunt Janelle, my daddy's sister, was our foster mother while Morgan took over the roll as my mother and father. It's funny, from time to time, I can smell my mother's scent. I always smell it when I am going through some mess. It's comforting and assuring and I feel as though she is protecting me. Lord, I hope she didn't see that shit with Marcy. I am sure both my parents have turned over five times in their graves. Thanks to Morgan, I never knew what it was like to grow up without a mother figure. I never had to worry about a thing, which is probably why I cling to her the way that I do. She will make a wonderful mother; she had a lot of experience dealing with my ass.

I got home an hour before Arthur's arrival, no thanks to Chas. He wasn't going to be satisfied until we went three hours of straight fucking today. Hell, asking what I had planned, shit, if I had anything planned, he done fucked it up now. My ass is so damn sore. After my shower, I try to clean a little bit. Arthur and Chas were right, this place is a sty. I can't believe I lived like this for four days, just to make people feel sorry for me. Oh well, a girl does what she has to do. I was determined to make Morgan resent telling me that she would talk to me when she was ready. So I took a few sick days from work, ordered pizza and leaving the cartons all over the place, half full 'cause I don't eat no damn pizza, and not bathing for days. Now that was truly a hard task. I started smelling my own ass after day one, but just as I've always believed, anything goes when you are trying to make a point. Arthur and Chas fell for it, but Morgan didn't. That bitch is too smart for her own good.

"Oh shit!" I exclaimed, opening my front door to see Arthur standing there as I was about to toss the garbage down the chute. "You scared the shit out of me."

Standing there with a smile on his face, "Sorry, Ray. Didn't mean to startle you."

"It's okay. Go on in and have a seat, I need to throw out the trash," I said, making my way to the chute at the end of the hallway. "Can I get you anything?" I closed the door behind me and headed towards the kitchen to pour myself a glass of apple juice.

"I see you've cleaned up. No thanks, I am fine. I don't have much time. Morgan is home patiently waiting for me to return. We are going to catch a movie tonight."

I take a seat beside him on the sofa. "Does she know you came to see me?"

"No. I told her that I got an emergency call from the hospital." Looking down at the floor and twiddling his thumbs, "What do you have in mind, Ray?"

"Well, let's just say that, when I am done, Ramone will be sorry he fucked around with me in the first place, and Renee will have a clear message to leave you the hell alone." I took a sip of my apple juice.

Massaging the back of his neck, "I don't want anyone to get hurt, Ray. I just want Renee to have a clear understanding that I don't want her."

"Don't worry, Arthur. I am not going to harm a hair on Renee or Ramone's head. However, I am not going to tell you what my plans are. Instead, I am going to tell you what I need you to do to ensure that my plan goes off without a hitch." I placed my hand on his knee.

"Okay, what do you need me to do?"

"Something very simple. All I need you to do is agree to see her." I stroked his knee.

"Agree to see her!" He jumped to his feet.

"Yes. Agree to see her." I watched him pace the floor.

"But why? I told you I didn't want to have anything to do with her."

"Yes, you told me that. But Arthur, in order to make my plan work, I need Renee away from her house for a few hours." He is going to wear a damn groove in my carpet.

Arthur peers out the window. "No. I can't do that. Sorry, Ray. You will have to come up with another plan."

Pulling myself up from the sofa and walking towards him, I grab him by his wrist. "Arthur, I understand where you are coming from, but this is what I need you to do. I am not asking you to go and have an affair with her. I am simply asking that you call her and ask her out on a date."

"No. I don't want to be caught in public with that crazy bitch!"

"Who says you have to be in public with her?"

"Well what do you suggest I do with her? Take her to a hotel or something?

"No, don't be silly. Why don't you take her for a drive to the Baltimore Harbor or somewhere? Hell, you can drive her ass to the fucking Shenandoah Valley for all I care, just get the bitch out of the damn house. Now, I am doing as you asked, why can't you do as I ask?"

"Okay, I will drive her around for a few hours, but that's it! Nothing more, understand?" He spoke in an authoritative tone that I seriously doubt he uses with Morgan.

Sensing that he might change his mind and not go along with my plan, caressing his face with the palms of my hands, "Arthur, listen to me baby. It's going to be okay. I will take care of Renee for you. I promise you that you will never, ever have to deal with her again. Do you trust that I can take care of things for you?"

"Yes, I do." He gazed into my eyes. "But..."

"Shh, don't say a word. Just know that Raven is here for you." I pressed my lips against his without the least bit of hesitation. To my surprise—well, not really, because all men are dogs, even my sister's husband—pulling me closer to him, Arthur slips his tongue in my mouth. As my tongue dances with his, I unzip his zipper and stroke his dick. While his tongue was playing inside of my mouth with intense force, he grabs the top of my head and guides me to a place that will give him ultimate pleasure. Kneeling before him, Arthur unleashes his sword and rams it in my mouth with deep, forceful thrusts. Caressing him with one hand and stroking under his testicles with the other, my finger finds its way to his asshole. Slowly inserting my finger, Arthur tightens his grip.

"Oh shit, what are you doing?"

"Open up for me baby. Just relax, Arthur." He loosens his grip on my finger. With the stroking of my finger, combined with the suction of my jaws, he comes to full climax in my mouth.

Arthur looks down at me with fear in his eyes. "What the fuck did we just do, Raven?"

My eyes locked with his. "We are doing what we've always wanted to do, Arthur. I am giving you pleasure and now, it's your turn to return the favor."

Looking at the ceiling with his mouth open, Arthur begins to cry. "Morgan! What about Morgan?"

Rising to my feet, I grab his face and pull it closer to mine. "Morgan doesn't suck your dick the way I just did, does she?"

Looking into my eyes, he replied, "No, she doesn't." Pulling me closer to him, he whispers in my ear. "We can't do this again and Morgan must never find out or I will kill you."

Wiggling from his grip, I take a step back and stare into his eyes. "You will not have to kill me because I do not plan to tell Morgan. Okay?"

Tucking in his shirt, he zipped up his pants and adjusted himself. "Yeah, okay."

My dream finally came true. Now Morgan is not the only one with Arthur. I have him too. Grabbing him by the hand, "Good. Come with me." I lead him towards my bedroom.

Following with hesitation, "Where are we going?"

Looking over my shoulder, "To my bedroom."

Coming to a complete halt, he jerks me towards him, "What the fuck for?"

"If you don't want Morgan to know about you fucking my mouth with your dick, you need to finish handling your business. Besides, look at it as being payment for getting Renee out of your life."

"Payment?"

"Yeppers! You see, nothing in this world is free, especially my services."

"Damn you, whore!"

"Call me what you want Arthur, so long as you call me with your dick in my pussy. Now, let's go or I will pick up that phone so fucking fast to call Morgan, it will make your fucking head spin."

"You wouldn't do that to your sister."

"No? You think I wouldn't? What makes you think I won't? After all, I just finished sucking her husband's dick."

"Ray, this is not right!"

"Well, I think it's too late for that, don't you? Besides, you should have resisted my kiss, but you didn't. Therefore, you wanted me just as much as I wanted you."

"No, that's not true."

"Yes, I think so. Arthur, for years I've seen how you look at me like a damn salivating dog."

"No, Ray, that is not true. I've only looked at you as a sister and nothing more."

"Yeah, whatever Arthur. Listen, let's just face it, you want me and I sure as hell want you. I've wanted you from the first time Morgan introduced us. I should have been with you, not her. She doesn't deserve you, Arthur. She doesn't know how to treat you, how to love you. You just said it yourself that she doesn't know how to suck dick. Now, let's stop wasting time."

Looking confused, he nodded towards the bedroom and followed me. Closing the door behind me, I remove my clothes. "Take off your clothes, Arthur. You are about to experience the best fuck you will ever have in your life." Three ejaculations later, Arthur dresses and slowly walks towards the front door, I follow behind him. "Arthur, this is our secret. You have my word."

Turning to face me, in a robotic tone of voice, "When do I call Renee?"

Walking up to him, I grab his crotch and gently stroke what now belongs to me. "Have her meet you at eight o'clock tomorrow night. I don't care where, as long as she is out of the house. I don't want Ramone to have any problems getting out."

Arthur stares past me in a daze. "Sure."

Increasing my grip on his dick, through clinched teeth, "Arthur, this belongs to me and Morgan. I don't want that bitch smelling my dick. If you fuck her, you will regret it."

"Sure."

27 / *be careful what you ask for...*

I just sold my soul to the devil herself. Sitting at a red light behind a car that is covered with bumper stickers, one catches my eye that says 'life's a bitch and then you die.' I'm ready to die. Everything that I've worked so hard for, is wasting away at the hands of that bitch. I can't believe I fucked my wife's sister. She had so much control over me, I felt like a straight bitch. Hell, I can't blame it all on Raven. Yes, she made advances towards me, but I accepted them. When she put her hand on my knee, I should've gotten the hell out of there. But damn, I honestly took it as being innocent. You know, between a sister and brother. Hell, I feel like I just committed incest. Maybe she was right, I wanted her as much as she wanted me. Whatever the case, it was wrong, but I enjoyed it.

Picking up my cell phone, I call Morgan to tell her that I've gotten held up at the hospital and that I would be home late. She will be disappointed because she really wanted to go to the movies, but I can't face her now. We will have to catch a movie tomorrow. Being the wife of a doctor, she is used to our plans changing at the drop of a hat. Trying to rub the tension from my neck, I make a detour to Roscoe's. I need a drink.

"Hi Dr. C., your usual table?" Shelly greeted me with her usual smile and friendly personality.

"Yes Shelly, thank you." She led me to my corner table in the shadows of the bar. I prefer to watch people instead of having them watch me.

"Your usual?" She placed a cocktail napkin in front of me. I nodded my head in agreement. With my head hung as low as it can hang, I try to relax and temporarily clear my mind of the visions of Raven sitting on top of me, riding me like I was a bull and she was the matador. I feel someone standing over me. Raising my head, thinking that it could be Shelly returning with my drink, I see Renee standing over me in a blazing red, low cut, thigh high dress.

"Well, well, well. Look who I've bumped into."

I am not in the mood to deal with another woman. "Hi."

Taking the seat across from me, Renee looks at me with confusion. "Why do you look like you've just lost your puppy?"

"What do you want? Why won't you leave me alone?"

"Question number one, I want you. Question two, because I want you."
She leaned in towards me, placing her hand over mine.

I jerked my hand away. "No, you don't want me, you want to fuck around on your husband."

"Well, that too," she chuckled.

"This isn't funny, Renee. You are trying to ruin my life and that ain't cool," I said with a snarl.

"Ruin your life? Don't be silly. I only want to enhance it. After all, wifey is pregnant, right? Therefore, I know you are not getting regular bedroom action. Hell, I'm helping her out."

"Oh?" I raised my head and stared into her eyes. "You want to tell me just how in the fuck you are helping out my wife by trying to fuck her husband?" I want to slap this bitch back to reality.

"By relieving her of her duties until she is capable of performing them again, which will be in about nine months, right?"

"I see. What makes you think she is not capable?"

"Arthur, I have two children, been there, done that. I didn't want Ramone to touch my ass because my hormones were running like hell, and he didn't want to touch me either, which is why he relieved me of my duties for the duration of each pregnancy."

"Humph, well you don't look pregnant to me. He must've lost track of time." I leaned back in my chair with Raven's words tossing around in my head. "Listen, you got any plans tomorrow night?"

"Nope. I'm as free as a bird."

"Good. Let's hook up around seven-thirty."

"Sounds good to me. Where?"

"Here." I looked at the whore with disgust. "I'll be back, I've gotta take a piss." I left the table and walked towards the bathroom. Entering the bathroom stall, I pull out my cell phone and dial Ray's number.

"Hello," came from a raspy voice.

"Its me."

"Oh, hello, baby. You want seconds?"

"It's done. I'm meeting Renee tomorrow at seven-thirty."

"Good."

Hanging up the phone before she could say another word, I return the phone to my inside jacket pocket, turn towards the toilet, unzip my pants and pull out my dick to take a piss. Washing my hands, the bathroom door opens. "Hey baby, I was getting worried about you. Thought I would come in and make sure you hadn't fallen in."

"No. Just finishing up." I grabbed a paper towel to wipe my hands.

"No, you are just getting started." She walked towards me, lifted up her dress, and propped her ass up on the sink. Damn, not again, Ray just wore my ass out. Knowing what she wanted, I knelt down before her, pulled the crotch of her panties to the side and commenced to tasting her.

"Suck that clit baby."

Thinking that my dick was exhausted, to my surprise, I feel a rise in my pants. Renee wraps her legs around my head and begins to forcefully fuck my face. "Oh yeah! I'm about to cum!" Grabbing on to her hips, not allowing her to pull away from me, I suck her clit with force, using my teeth to nibble as hard as I could without causing permanent damage. "Damn baby, not so hard," she flinched. Not hearing her, I suck and bite harder and harder. With visions of Ray dancing through my head, I yank Renee down from the sink, turn her ass towards me, bend her over with force, unzip my pants, tear her panties from her body, spread her cheeks and ram my dick inside her. "Ouch! Oh my God! Take it easy, Arthur. That's the wrong hole!"

"I thought this was what you wanted. You want to be fucked by Dr. Arthur Carrington, right? You wanted to relieve my wife of her duties for nine months, right? Well, this is how I fuck my wife, so get used to being fucked in your ass for nine months, you trick ass whore. Now, shut the fuck up and let me do my business." I said between clinched teeth, watching her distorted face in the mirror. "You should watch what you ask for Renee, you just might get it."

After ejaculating inside her, I retrieve my dick, grab a paper towel, wipe her off and toss her where she belongs, in the fucking trash. "I've got to run. I will see you at seven-thirty sharp, tomorrow night. Don't wear no underwear and bring lubricant. I don't like pulling skin when going in your tight ass. Are we clear?" I looked at Renee with disgust.

With her ass still in the air, her face covered with tears that dripped in the yellow-stained sink, "Yes, I understand."

28 / it's on

I paged Ramone at six o'clock. The sorry bastard has no clue what he is in for, neither does his trick ass wife. Fucking with two people who mean the world to me, just don't fly in my book. Now that Morgan is pregnant, it will be my responsibility to take care of Arthur, until Morgan is ready to perform her wifely duties again. That's why I have to get that whore, Renee, out of the picture, as well as her nasty ass husband. I can only handle Chas and Arthur. I'm good, but I ain't no Superwoman. Gathering my things and stuffing them into a satchel, my phone rings. I hope that's Ramone so we can get the show on the road. The excitement of it all is really making me horny. Assuming its him, not checking caller ID, I answer the phone. "Hey baby."

"Hi baby," Chas said.

"Hey boo. How are you?" I tried to mask my disappointment.

"I'm fine, but I'm missing you baby."

"Oh baby, I miss you too. What's up?"

"I want to see you tonight."

"Sure. But it will have to be later. I'm meeting with Morgan this evening."

"Really? That's great. You guys are finally going to make up."

"Yeah, thanks to Arthur. I just love him so much."

"That's wonderful baby. What are you two going to do?"

"Um, I am going out to their place and we're going to have drinks and talk. You know, girl stuff."

"Okay, well, what time will you be finished?" My call waiting beeps in my ear.

"Baby, I've got to run. I will see you around ten o'clock, okay?"

"Okay baby, have fun."

I clicked over to my second line. "Well, hello stranger. It's been a while since I've seen your number pop up in my pager."

"Yes, well, a girl has been quite busy."

"Yeah, I bet. Chas has been keeping you tied up, huh?"

"What?"

"Don't play dumb with me girl," he said chuckling. "But, it's cool. It ain't like we married or we're an item or anything. You can fuck who you wanna fuck."

"Well, I'm trying to fuck you. You got any plans for tonight?"

"It depends."

"On what?"

"On what you got planned in that pretty little head of yours."

"How about me, you and a hotel room?"

"What about Chas?"

"What about him?"

"Oh, so it's like that?"

"Like what? Look, you know how I roll, free as a bird."

"I hear that. What's wrong with your place?"

"What's wrong with yours?" I snapped.

"What hotel?"

"No, for real. What's wrong with your place?" I gave him the opportunity to come clean once and for all. "Ramone, why haven't you invited me to your place?

"Huh?"

"You didn't understand the question?"

"Uh, well baby, I'm a little ashamed of my place. It's not in a good area for one and it's not presentable. I will be moving soon, so when I move, you will be the first guest." This fucker is lying through his teeth.

"Is that right? Well, I've made reservations for us, under your name, at the Renaissance across from the Washington Convention Center."

"Cool. What time?"

"How about eight o'clock?"

"Fine."

"Excellent. Just go to the front desk and check-in. I've already paid for the room. Get the key, relax yourself and I will arrive around eight-thirty."

"Sounds good. It's a quarter past seven now, so let me run. Listen, I can't stay overnight."

"Yes, I know." I slammed the phone in its cradle. Tell me something I don't know motherfucker. Making sure everything is going according to plan, I call Arthur to confirm that he has not chickened out on me. Since I didn't get an answer from his cell or office phone, I make a bold move and call the house phone.

"Hey Morgan, it's me."

"Yeah, I know who it is," she said, irritably.

"Morgan, are you still upset with me?"

Morgan took a deep sigh. "What do you want, Raven? What of 'don't call me, I'll call you' that you don't understand?"

"I wanted to tell you that I'm sorry and I love and miss you dearly. Mo, I want my sister back!" Now, if she believes this shit, I've got some swamp land in Florida to sell. I do love her, but I don't miss her funky attitude.

"Raven, you come with too much stress and I can't deal with that right now. My baby can't take the stress."

"I know, I know and I will do whatever I have to do to relieve the stress. If you don't want me calling you anymore, then I won't. But, I just want you to know that I'm truly sorry, I have taken responsibility for my actions and, from now on, I will clean up my own mess."

"That's mighty big of you, Raven," she said in a nasty kind of way.

"It's the truth, Morgan," I pleaded with crossed fingers and toes. If I were superstitious, I would cross my legs too.

"I believe you, Ray. Let's just take it one step at a time, alright?"

"Alright!" I pretended to sound excited. "Can we do lunch or something?"

"Sure. Maybe next week."

"Great! Oh, is Arthur there?"

"Yes he is, why?" She is so damn nosey. Sometimes I can't stand this moody ass wench. She needs to get over it. Taking a drag from my blunt, I try to maintain my cool and hold my tongue. "I wanted to thank him for talking to me and helping me see what you've been trying to get me to see for the longest." I hoped that she believed that bullshit 'cause I sure as hell didn't mean it.

"Well, that's good, Ray. Hold on, I'll get Arthur for you," she said, placing her hand over the receiver and yelling for Arthur to pick up the phone.

"Dr. Carrington," came from a groggy voice. He sounded like he was knocked out, so I waited for Morgan to hang up the phone before I responded.

"Arthur, are you asleep?"

"Just taking a nap." He obviously is not aware of who he is talking to.

"Arthur!" I shouted. "Get your ass up and ready to meet Renee. Man, it is after seven-thirty!"

"Raven, you don't have to yell. I'm not meeting her until eight o'clock. I'll leave out shortly."

"Okay, fine. Don't chicken out on me."

"I won't. Besides, Renee has been blowing up my pager."

"Good. That's good. Oh, and Arthur?"

"Yes," he said through a yawn.

"I want you to arrange to have rounds at the hospital this week. Better yet, make one of them an overnighter. I have an itch you need to scratch and Morgan isn't the only one who would like to wake up to your face."

"Raven, we can't do that again, I'm sorry. I love my wife, your sister, how could you do this to her?"

"Man, you must be out yo damn mind. If you loved Morgan, you wouldn't be sniffing Renee's drawers nor would you have shoved your dick in my mouth. So, don't hand me that bullshit."

"Ray, I..."

"What?" I interjected. "What in the hell do you have to say?"

"I love my wife."

"No! You don't love Morgan, you love me. You've always loved me. I've always been the one you wanted, but she got in the way. So now I have you, even if it means that I have to share you. I don't mind sharing you with my sister, just not with anyone else," I said with a snarl. "So Arthur, how does it feel to have two wives? I'm sure you'll enjoy switching up beds from time to time."

"Raven, you are sick!" he snarled through clenched teeth, while looking out the bedroom door to make sure Morgan was nowhere in earshot.

"Tell me I'm lying, Arthur." There was dead silence. Arthur didn't say shit, which is just what I expected. "Uh huh, just as I thought."

"I do love Morgan." He sounded faint.

"Whatever you say, Arthur. But, you just remember one thing, when my dear, sweet sister isn't in the mood to open her legs or her mouth, you know who will. Of course, you will have to share me with Chas," I chuckled. "It's going to be a nice mix. Chas can eat the pussy and you have the big dick. Now, get your ass up and go meet the bitch so I can take care of my business. I expect to see you tomorrow night." I hung up the phone not giving him a chance to utter his last plea to end our new found union. Arthur will soon realize that I'm doing him and Morgan a favor. I'm going to help her keep her husband. Hell, he is no different than the other dogs out here roaming the streets, he thinks with his dick too. So, to keep his black ass out of trouble, when he feels the urge to explore other territory, he will come to me instead. That way, we are keeping it in the family, which is how it should be, and everyone will be happy, even Arthur. He may not realize that now, but he will.

Walking through the lobby of the Renaissance, I ask the Concierge to point me in the direction of the bathroom. Inside the bathroom stall, I strip to my birthday suit and oil myself down with sesame oil. Neatly folding my clothes, placing them on the back of the toilet, I remove the sheer silk robe from my satchel bag. After slipping on my robe and my four-inch pumps, I repack the neatly folded clothes into the satchel and make my way to Room 620. I feel like Foxy Brown; ready to kick some ass.

"Damn baby, you look good. You are truly a sight for sore eyes."

Handing Ramone my satchel, I untie my robe and let it drop to the floor. Standing in the hallway, butt-naked, I take a step backwards and motion for Ramone to join me.

"Oh, you want to play games, huh? That's my girl," he said with a smirk on his face, following my lead.

"Nope, I'm done playing games with you, Ramone. This shit is for real," I said, turning my back to face him and bending over. "Stroke my ass with your tongue."

"Stroke your what with my what? You want me to do it right here, in the hallway?"

"Hell yeah," I said, facing him. "Let me find out your ass has turned into a little bitch all of a sudden."

"Naw, it ain't like that. But damn baby, right here in the hallway?" Ramone walked towards me and tugged on my arm. "Baby, let's take this inside."

"I don't believe this fucking shit!" I yelled, jerking away from his grasp. "You weren't scared when you sucked my ass in the doorway of my condo. Because of your antics, I got in trouble with my housing association. So motherfucker, the way I see it, you owe me. Now, when I turn my ass around and bend over, I want your nose smelling my crack. Got it?"

"Alright. I can play it your way, Ray." He looked at me like I had just lost my ever-loving mind. Grabbing my arm and spinning me around, Ramone bends me over, spreads my cheeks and strokes my hole with his tongue. With a hard smack to my ass, "Is this what the fuck you want?"

With force, Ramone rams three fingers inside me. "Damn baby, not so rough. You're gonna make me sore before we get started good. Let's take it slow." I feel just like I felt that day in the elevator with Jay. I must maintain control. Rising up and facing Ramone, I ram my tongue in his mouth, forcefully kissing him while trying to walk our way into the room. Ramone wasn't having it. "Oh, hell no, Ms. I Don't Want Everybody In My Business. We are going to take care of your business right here."

"But baby, I have plans."

"What kind of plans?" He looked at me as if he could tell that I was going to lie out my ass.

"This is your night, Ramone. I want it to be seductive for you." I mentally cross my fingers, because physically, he has my hands in, what felt like, a chokehold.

"Oh, now you're talking. Well, come on in. You want to seduce Ramone, huh?"

"Yeah, that's right baby." I walked into the room and glanced at him over my shoulder.

"Well, instead of seducing Ramone, why don't you pretend that I'm Chas and seduce me the way you would seduce him."

"Okay, if that's what you want." I search my mind to find a way to regain control, because right now, Ramone has total control. "Come here baby, lay down on the bed. Let me give you a massage."

"Do you give Chas massages?" He removed his shirt and threw it onto the tethered burnt orange-colored chair that's the same color as the walls, carpet and curtains. Okay, all of this orange puts me in the mood for a Chicago hot dog and one of those slushy drinks from the Orange Julius in Landover Mall.

"Isn't that what you want?" I walk over to him, unzip his pants, allow them to drop to the floor. "Lay face down on the bed baby, let Raven work out those kinks." I kissed him on his lips.

Walking over to my satchel bag, I bend over to retrieve the baby oil. Ramone starts to run his damn mouth. "Damn, you giving all that ass to Chas? That motherfucker knows he can't handle that shit. Hell, he knows that he ain't no damn Ramone. Why that punk trying to fill my shoes?"

"You're right, Chas is definitely no Ramone." The fact that Ramone is talking about my man, doesn't sit well with me, which is why I'm about to light that ass up. Glancing over my shoulder to make sure Ramone's eyes are somewhere other than on me, I remove the strap-on dildo from the satchel and toss it over towards the bed. Luckily, it landed on the floor. After tying his wrists and ankles to the bedposts with silk scarves I purchased from Woolworth's 5 & 10¢ store, I squirt baby oil all over his back, concentrating on his ass. I want to make sure this bitch is nicely greased. Straddling him, I gently massage his back, stroke his ass and insert my finger in and out of his hole. Leaning on his back, I whisper into his ear. "Baby, keep your face down in the pillow, I have a surprise for you."

After Ramone nods in agreement, I reach down beside the bed, grab the dildo and strap it around my waist. Rubbing baby oil on the dildo, I'm enraged at the thought of Ramone fucking me for damn near three years and never telling me about his wife. Easing my finger in and out of his hole, I spread his cheeks apart. "Arghhhhhhh! What the fuck are you doing?" he yelled, with pain from me ramming the dildo in his hole.

"Fucking you in your ass, just like you've been fucking me in mine for years. Now, shut the fuck up and enjoy it," I yelled.

"Raven, I'm gonna fuck you up, bitch!" He tried to wiggle free of the harnesses that held him bound to the bed. "I never fucked you in your ass because you wouldn't let me!"

"I don't particularly care for being fucked in my ass, Ramone. Does Renee?" I intensify my strokes with each spoken word.

"Arghhhhhhh! You fucking bitch! I'm gonna kill you!" he yelled, still trying to wiggle free.

"Shut the fuck up!" I slapped him upside his head with all my might. "You deserve to be fucked in your ass, you bastard! How dare you climb in and out of my fucking bed, for three fucking years, and not tell me that your fucking ass is fucking married. You chose the wrong bitch to fuck with, Ramone. You've done what you wanted to do to me, for three years. You've fucked me any way you wanted to fuck me, for three years. Now, you bastard, it's my turn to fuck you the way I want. And, I choose to fuck you straight in your ass, you faggot ass bitch!" I screamed, outraged with Ramone's ass, fucking another bitch while fucking me. Hearing his cries and noticing that blood has formed around the dildo, I refuse to cease stroking. He hasn't suffered enough. "Shut up!" I exclaimed, striking a blow to the back of his head.

"You better kill me, bitch, 'cause if I get loose…"

"Are you threatening me? Keep talking shit. The more you talk, the more I push, and the more I push, the more I want to cum. The more I thrust this dildo in Ramone's hole, the more it stimulates my clit. "Damn, this shit is feeling good. Now I see what you dog's get out of fucking us in our asses."

"A bitch deserves to be fucked in her ass, and as soon as I get free, I am going to do just that to your ass, you cunt!"

"Why don't you just shut the fuck up so I can get my orgasm?" I smacked him upside his head, again. "Damn, for once, will you please let me get my orgasm!" Ramone is yelling to the top of his lungs. I continue to thrust, faster and harder. "Yes, yes, yes!" I yell, as my body goes limp on Ramone's oily back. Dismounting him, I walk over to the phone to dial Renee's cell phone number. "Listen to me you faggot motherfucker, you tell that bitch wife of yours to meet you here in thirty minutes."

"Suppose I don't?"

Anger rises inside of me from his response. Out of nowhere, I hit him clear upside his head with the phone. "Well, if you don't, I will just have to light that ass up again. You like that shit, huh?"

"Naw, I don't like that shit, you trick ass whore!" He spat his hatred of me in my face.

Wiping the saliva from my face, I stand over him, adjust the dildo and straddle his back again. "Seems like you like this shit to me." I spread his cheeks apart and squirt the remaining bottle of baby oil in the crack of his ass.

"No! Raven, no! Please don't!" he pleaded with tears running down his face. "Okay, I'll call her. I will do whatever you want."

"Good." I reach for the phone and dial Renee's cell phone number. "Stop that fucking crying. That shit is getting on my last nerve."

29 / if it walks like a dog, barks like a dog and wag it's tail like a dog...it's a dog

Standing in the archway of the bathroom, with a white cotton towel wrapped around my waist, Renee kneels before me, taking me inside her mouth. "Lady, I can't take anymore. You have worn a brotha out," I said, pressing the palm of my hand against her forehead to push her away from my soft dick. "Quit, that tickles," I chuckled.

"I can't help it baby. You are addictive."

"Yeah, whatever. At least, let me catch my breath."

"Alright. I'll give you ten minutes and then I want a repeat performance." She rose to her feet, moving me to the side. Looking over her shoulder, "I'm thirsty, how about ordering a bottle of champagne. We need to celebrate." She closed the bathroom door behind her.

"Celebrate what?"

"Us," she said, between the splatter of urine hitting the toilet water.

"What kind of champagne do you like?"

"Will you stop talking through that damn door and come in here," she said, flushing the toilet.

"No thanks. I'll wait until you're finished doing whatever it is that you're doing." I call Room Service and order a bottle of Cristal.

"I'm hungry, order some food too," she yelled through the closed door.

"And two lobsters with a cheese and fruit platter. Thanks."

"Yummy. Cris and lobster, what a classy combination." She exited the bathroom as I was placing the phone back in its cradle. "You really know how to treat a girl." She wrapped her arms around my neck and kissed my lips.

"Well, I do aim to please." I stroked her naked body. "Aren't you going to answer that?"

"Answer what?"

"Your cell phone."

"Why?"

"Because...it's ringing?"

"Oh, I don't want to answer it," she whined with pouted lips, in a baby's voice.

"It may be your kids. Answer the phone woman." I smacked her on her ass.

Reluctantly, Renee snatches her purse from the oak-carved, colonial desk and retrieves her cell phone. "Hey baby, it's me. Listen, I have a room at the Renaissance. I want you to meet me here in thirty minutes. Hurry up baby, I need you."

"Why do you have a room at the Renaissance, Ramone?"

"Listen baby, don't ask any questions. Just come, please."

"What's going on? Why all of a sudden you want me?"

"I'm sorry, okay? I know I haven't been the best husband, but I'm ready to make things right between us. Please baby, give me a chance."

"Well, I'm busy right now. I'll call you back," she barked. "What's your room number?"

"Baby, wait, no. Please, I need you, come now."

"Ramone, okay, I said I was busy. What is your room number and I will call you right back!"

"Room 620. Please baby, call me back."

"I will, damn." She ended the call and tossed the cell phone on the matching oak-carved colonial nightstand. "Now, where were we, baby?"

"What was that about?"

"Oh nothing, just Ramone. It's funny, he has a room at the Renaissance."

"Renee, we are at the Renaissance."

"No shit, Sherlock. Now, where were we?" Renee walks towards me and reaches out and begins to caress my soft, limp dick. "Ooh, looks like you need a little help down there." She kneels in front of me and takes me inside her mouth.

I push her head away from my torso. "Renee, why is Ramone in this hotel?" Damnit. Of all the hotels in Washington, D.C., why in the hell did Ray have to choose this hotel? "This is too close," I mumbled.

"What's that, baby?"

"Oh, nothing. Just wondering where the hell is that Room Service. I'm going to hop in the shower baby. Sign for the Room Service for me, okay?"

"Sure baby, but I don't know why you are going to take a shower because you are just going to get all pussied-up again," she chuckled.

Walking past her, "Just sign for it." I tap her on the ass and make my way into the bathroom. "I won't be long." I close and lock the door behind me. After pacing the bathroom floor for a bit, I turn on the shower. What the hell is Raven doing here? I thought she was going to initiate her plan at Ramone's place, at least that is what I figured. Hell, that is why she asked me to get Renee out of the house, isn't it? Damn, now I am fucked. If Raven finds out that I am in a hotel, fucking Renee, she will make my life miserable. Why would Ramone call for Renee to come to the room? What does Raven have planned for Renee?

Renee knocks on the bathroom door, startling me. "Arthur, you okay?"

"Yes. Yes, I am fine."

"Okay, the champagne is here."

"Okay, I will be out in a minute."

"Would you like some company? I could bring the champagne in there and we could pick up where we left off, in the shower."

"No, no. I will be out."

"Okay, well hurry up. I miss you already." She walked over to the oak-carved cocktail table to pour the champagne. "Damn, everything in this bitch is oak-carved."

"What's that?" I yelled from the bathroom.

"Nothing, just talking to myself."

"Just don't answer yourself," I chuckled, exiting the bathroom and walking towards her.

"You're not dripping wet, did you take a shower?"

"Uh, no, I didn't. You were right, why take a shower when I am going to get, how you say, 'pussied-up' again."

"Absolutely, we still have unfinished business to take care of."

"Renee, you have worn me out. We have christened every inch of this hotel room. I think I have a bruise on my butt cheek from you straddling me on the corner of the night stand."

"Aw, come here and let me kiss it for you and make it all better," she said with her lips poked out and making the kissing noise.

"Haha! Oh, you really want to kiss my ass, huh?"

"If that is what it's going to take to get your private to stand at attention, then, absolutely."

"You know Renee, you are really something."

"What do you mean?" She took a sip of Cristal.

"I've had a wonderful time with you this evening."

"See, I told you that you wouldn't be disappointed."

"Yeah, I know. Which makes me wonder why your husband doesn't realize what he has in you."

"Oh, he knows. I think it's more of being tired of the same routine and wanting to have his cake and eat it too. Ramone is a good father, but he sucks at being a husband and a friend."

"Oh, I see. Well, are you going to call him back?"

"Yeah, I will. But it will be on my terms. So Arthur, now that you've been with me, how do you feel about your wife?"

"What kind of question is that? I love my wife."

"You do?"

"Yes. As a matter of fact, I love my wife dearly."

"Then why are you here with me?"

"Renee, don't spoil a good evening, okay?"

"No, really. We need to communicate. We need to discuss what our expectations are of each other."

"I don't know why I am here."

"Okay, so what is this?"

"What is what?"

"This? Us?"

"There is no 'us' and 'this' is just sex. Nothing more, nothing less."

"Suppose I want more."

"I will not be able to accommodate you."

"Sure you can. You've already done it." She walked towards me and sat on my lap. "Arthur, the way you made love to me was so passionate and loving. You wanted and needed it just as much as I did."

Looking into her eyes, trying to find truth in what she was saying. "Yes, I suppose I did. But, don't get me wrong, Renee, there is nothing that you've done here tonight that my wife does not do. I'm not here because I am unhappy or dissatisfied with Morgan, I am here because you intrigued me and, yes, this is what I wanted. But I also know that this, whatever this is, will not last forever. We must keep things in perspective."

30 / never let a dog suffer, it's inhumane

I hung up the phone and pat Ramone on his head. "Now, while we are waiting for your whorish ass wife, who likes to pick up married men in bars, I'm going to take a shower. The smell of you makes me want to puke." I head towards the bathroom.

"Ray, aren't you going to untie me?"

"Do I look like a fucking fool to you?"

"Please Ray, I'm in so much pain."

"Good!"

"Please Ray."

"Ramone, I don't give a rat's ass if you're in pain."

Walking towards my satchel, I retrieve my .22-caliber from its holster. Standing over him, I stare into his eyes that are flooded with fear and tears. Squatting to bring myself face-to-face with my prey, "Ramone, did you really think that you could get away with lying to me?"

"Ray, please don't kill me," he cried. "I was wrong for not telling you about Renee, but I didn't think it would've made a difference. You said you only wanted the dick and nothing more," he said through sobs.

"Ramone, you hurt me. I gave myself to you for three years. You did things to me that I would've never allowed anyone to do to me. You brought another man into my home to fuck me while you watched."

"But, I thought that was what you wanted?"

"It was and I enjoyed it immensely, which is why I am fucking your boy, Chas."

"Fuck Chas."

Waving my finger in his face, "Ooh, that's not very nice of you Ramone."

"Man, why did he have to go and tap my pussy?"

"Don't blame this shit on Chas. After all, you're the one who led the horse to the water."

"He will never be me."

"You're right, once again. Chas will never be like you because he has what you don't."

"Yeah, and what's that?"

"Me."

"Bitch, you are old news. Yeah, I had my way with you. I fucked you when and where I wanted. You the dumb bitch for allowing me to do that to your ass."

"I suggest you shut the fuck up," I said between clinched teeth.

"Yeah, I did what the fuck I wanted to do to you," he chuckled. "Remember the time I made you get on your knees and suck my dick in that pissy ass alley in Anacostia?" he laughed. 'Uh huh, and since we going back down memory lane, remember the time I took you over to my boy's crib and the fellas ran a train on your freak nasty ass?" he asked through uncontrollable laughter, sort of reminding me of the Joker from Batman & Robin.

"Yes, I remember." I stood over him.

"Yeah, I fucked your ass royally and you loved that shit. The only difference between you and those tricks on 14th and U Streets is that you do it for free, you dumb bitch!" he spat in my face. "Chas can have your used up ass. Your shit's been stretched so wide, it's like the fucking black hole." He laughed in my face. "You used to be tight, now my dick gets lost up in ya!"

Ramone's words stung deep and the blood running through my veins is now at its boiling point. My hands are shaking and my knees are feeling weak. Nevertheless, I maintain my cool. "Anything else you need to get off your chest, baby?" I asked, reaching for the pillow that lay beside Ramone's bruised head.

With uncontrollable laughter, barely getting his words out. "Yeah, does Arthur know that you and Morgan be swapping pussy juices?

"No. But I'll be sure to give him your regards." His body went limp from the muffled gun shot to the back of his head. "Look at what you made me do," I said to the blood stained pillow. "I told you to stop running your mouth."

"Ray, it is time for you to stand up and take responsibility for your own actions. I don't care how you do it, but you need to do it and do it without me." "Raven, do you ever take responsibility for your own actions?" "Ray, you don't think about anyone, but yourself."

"Stop, stop, stop!" I yelled, with my hands covering my ears. "Leave me alone!"

Feeling damn near close to being fitted for a straight jacket, I try to gather my composure. I need to clean this place up. What am I going to do with the body? Okay, calm down Raven, you can do this. I run to the bathroom, grab a towel and dampen it with hot, soapy water. I wipe down everything that I've touched, from the bed, to the nightstand, to the door knobs. I gathered all of my belongings, including the sheets from the bed. "Damn, where am I going to put this damn comforter?" I asked, but no one responded. I look in the closet for one of those plastic bags that you use to put your dirty clothes in and I neatly fold the comforter and place it inside the plastic bag.

Standing in the middle of the room, I look around, making sure that I haven't forgotten to wipe down something. Then it dawned on me that I touched Ramone's clothing. Snatching his clothing from the tethered burnt orange-colored chair, shoving them into my satchel, I head for the door. A knock at the door stops me in my tracks. Damn, who the fuck is that? Oh shit, Renee. Contemplating whether I should answer the door or not, being in the same room with Ramone's dead body is making me heave up this afternoon's turkey sandwich. The knock is persistent. "Ramone, it's Renee," came from the other side of the door. "Oh shit," I mouthed. After taking a peep through the peephole, standing behind the door, I slowly open the door.

"Ramone?" Renee walked through the door with caution. "Where are…," the sight of her husband's dead body stops her in her tracks. "Oh my God, Ramone!" She ran to his side as I slammed the door behind her, startling her.

"Hello Renee." I walk towards her and her dead husband. "Well, you finally made it. You almost missed me."

Renee took her stare off Ramone's corpse and directed it towards me. "Did you do this?"

"Naw, he did it to himself." I drop my hands to my side. "He was a bad boy, and well, he had to be punished."

Renee, standing there in shock, with her eyes moving from me, to the door, to the phone, looking confused. "If I were you, Renee, I would think twice about reaching for the phone or the door. My level of tolerance is very low, as you can see." I pointed at Ramone's corpse.

"But why? I don't understand."

"Sure you do. You understand fully. From what I hear, you know all about me."

"Raven Ward?"

"Live, in person and here to serve you."

"Huh?"

"Listen, the way I see it, you have three choices. One, I can keep you alive and spend the rest of my life behind bars for killing your two-timing husband, but we don't want that." I pull my .22-caliber from my satchel and walk towards the bed. "Two, I can have you lay face down beside him, place a pillow over your head and you two can spend the rest of eternity in hell." I pick up a pillow. "Three, I can have you lay face up on the bed, place the pillow over your face and shoot you in the head, then place the gun in your hand and call it a murder suicide."

"You are a crazy bitch!" she exclaimed. "You will never get away with this."

"Yada, yada, yada. What will it be? One, two or three?"

"I prefer four." With a high kick towards my face, Renee attempts to knock the gun from my hand, but she slips up, busting her ass on the floor and hits her head against the corner of the oak-carved night stand. Renee's body goes limp.

"Oh, you trying to be Jackie Chan on a sista, huh?" I grab that bitch by her weave and lift her to the bed, then lay her face up beside her beloved Ramone. The bitch should've taken a shower before she came in here, she smells like pussy, the nasty whore. "Well, Arthur fucked you after all," I said to her comatose body. "That wasn't the right the thing to do, Renee." I place the pillow over her face. "This is all Arthur's fault. I told him not to fuck you and he did it anyway. Enjoy hell bitch." I pull the trigger, firing a muffled gunshot to the side of Renee's head.

Using soap and water to wipe down the gun, I place the gun in Renee's hand. Removing the pillowcases and shoving them inside my satchel, I turn to walk out of the room, thinking to myself that it was a good thing I purchased that gun hot off the street. Who knows who it's registered to. I take one last glance over the room. I close the door behind me, coming face-to-face with Arthur. "What the…"

"Raven, what have you done?"

"What business is it of yours?"

"Where is Renee and Ramone?"

"Oh, so now you are concerned about Renee? I thought you wanted her out of the picture, Arthur?"

"Well, yes, but I didn't want any harm to come to her either."

"Ha! Too late for that, babe."

"What do you mean?"

"You shouldn't have fucked her, Arthur!"

"I didn't…"

"Yes you did! She reeks of cum! You sonofabitch! Did you think to use a fucking condom?

"Open the door, Raven."

"Arthur, I suggest you turn yourself around and go home to your wife, where you belong. It's your fault I did what I did."

"How is it my fault?"

I grabbed him by the crotch. "You gave up my dick and I thought we had an understanding."

"Listen, Raven…"

"No, you listen. You will go home to your wife, my sister, and you will be the loving husband that you've always been and you will keep your dick in check and never, ever do this shit again. I will go home, shower, relax and call Chas."

"What about us?"

"There never was an us, Arthur. You see, Morgan spoke so highly of the size of your dick and of your ability to perform in the bedroom, I wanted to see for myself. She wasn't lying, you do have a big dick and you are very good. Go home to your wife, Arthur, it's over."

"But…"

"Arthur, you are trying my patience."

"Ray, what about Renee?"

"What about her?"

"Well, suppose she decides to call Morgan and tell her everything?"

"Brother-in-law, you don't have to worry about Renee calling anyone."

"Why is that?"

"She's dead."

Arthur took a step backwards. "Oh my God!" He exclaimed.

I reached for the collar of his shirt and pulled him close to me. I could smell her pussy on his breath. "Shh. Keep your voice down."

"Why did you have to kill her?"

"I had no choice. It was either her or me…"

"But, you didn't have to end her life…" Arthur stared into space.

"I did what I had to do. Are you going to start trippin'? Do you want to join her?"

Arthur took a step backwards, looking me up and down. "You would, wouldn't you?

"Don't you know by now that, in my book, anything goes?"

about the author

Jessica Tilles is a native Washingtonian and *Anything Goes* is her debut novel. She is currently working on her second novel, *In My Sister's Corner*, to be released Spring 2003. She resides in Maryland with her husband and their two dogs. Visit Jessica at www.jessicatilles.com.

about the cover artist

Jon Bull is the founder of Joppa Graphix Ink., and a self-taught artist who enjoys and excels in a variety of artistic expressions, including sculptures, murals and comic illustrations. To learn more about Jon, visit www.jessicatilles.com.